A Carnival of Secrets

A Carnival of Secrets

Paul McCusker

PUBLISHING
Colorado Springs, Colorado

A CARNIVAL OF SECRETS

Library of Congress Cataloging-in-Publication Data
McCusker, Paul, 1958-
A carnival of secrets / Paul McCusker.
p. cm.—(Adventures in Odyssey; 12)
Summary: When Patti wins a stuffed bear at Odyssey's spring carnival, a series of strange events leads to a mystery and reunites her with her friend Mark who now lives in Washington, D.C.
ISBN 1-56179-546-1

[1. Friendship—Fiction. 2. Espionage—Fiction. 3. Conduct of life—Fiction. 4. Mystery and detective stories.] I. Title. II. Series: McCusker, Paul, 1958- Adventures in Odyssey; 12.
PZ7.M47841635Car 1997

[Fic]—DC21 97-10868
CIP
AC

Published by Focus on the Family Publishing, Colorado Springs, CO 80995.

The author is represented by the literary agency of Alive Communications, 1465 Kelly Johnson Blvd., Suite 320, Colorado Springs, CO 80920.

Editor: Larry K. Weeden
Front cover illustration: JoAnn Weistling

Printed in the United States of America

97 98 99 00/10 9 8 7 6 5 4 3 2 1

Adventures in Odyssey Novel 12:
A Carnival of Secrets

CHAPTER ONE

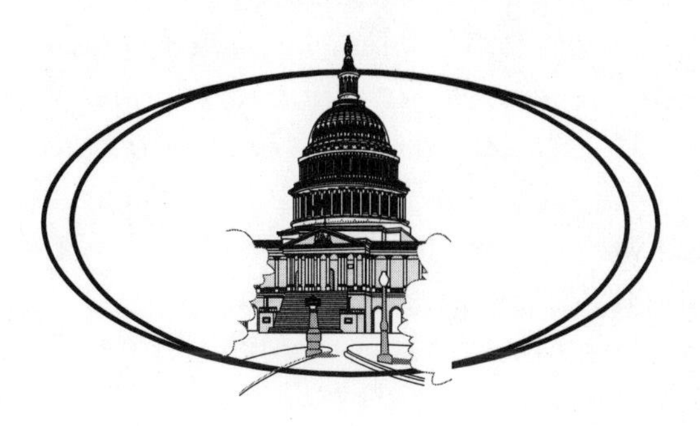

Dear Patti,

How are you? I am fine. Sorry it's taken me a long time to write, but I've been real busy since we moved back to Washington, D. C. I was going to call you, but Dad said I'd have to pay for the call, and I keep spending the money I mean to save up.

The cherry blossoms came out the other day, and Mom says she can't believe it's been over eight months since we moved back here. I think she misses Odyssey.

They are getting along. Mom and Dad, I mean. They don't fight as much as they used to, and when they do they make up fast. They are happy. They get all huggy-kissy a lot more now. I think the counselor is helping them.

Most of my old friends are still here, and we do things together just like before I moved to Odyssey.

We're having a blast. I even like being back in my old school. My teachers are cool. Mr. Nock (he's my math teacher) said that he thinks he visited Odyssey once when he got lost on his way to a convention somewhere. Mrs. Baker (she's my English teacher) read my "What I Did for Summer" essay and said she wished she could go to Odyssey sometime. I will give her your address in case she does.

How are Mr. Whittaker and Whit's End? I told my friends about it, and they didn't believe it's real. Maybe one day we'll rent a bus and I'll take them so they can see for themselves.

Sincerely yours,
Mark Prescott

Patti Eldridge threw herself back onto her bed with a heavy sigh. The bedsprings creaked in protest somewhere under the thick, pink comforter. The curved, wrought-iron headstand bumped against the wall with a thud. Patti stared up at the canopy. "Mark . . ." she groaned.

Patti had written to Mark Prescott almost every week since he had left Odyssey. That was last September. Had he written back in the eight months since? No. And when he finally did, it was *this*—a short note telling her how well he was doing.

A car drove past the front of the house. The morning sun hit the chrome, sending a reflection that moved like a white phantom across Patti's forest green walls. She frowned. Even the walls reminded her of Mark. He had painted her room while she was in the hospital, nursing a concussion and broken arm. He'd painted it forest green because the two of them loved the story of Robin Hood so much. The car drove away. The phantom reflection chased after it, maybe to haunt other houses along the street.

Patti didn't know which was worse, that Mark had sent such a short note after all this time or that he seemed to be so happy. How could he be happy when she was miserable? How could he go back to his old life and old friends and leave her stuck in Odyssey by herself? It wasn't fair.

"We're supposed to be best friends," Patti said to her empty room. She remembered how Mark had moved to Odyssey at the beginning of last summer because his parents had separated. He and his mom had lived in his grandmother's house. Patti muttered, "He didn't have a single friend until I came along. I'm the one who took him to Whit's End and introduced him to Whit and showed him around Odyssey and . . ."

He had forgotten all about that, Patti was certain. *He moved back to Washington and forgot all about me,* she thought gloomily.

Rolling over onto her stomach, she rested her chin on her crossed arms and pouted. She'd never had a friend as close as Mark; not before he arrived in Odyssey, and certainly not since he left. *No wonder,* she thought. *Who wants to be friends with a tomboy?* The boys didn't like her because she was a girl, even though she liked being outside, playing sports, racing bikes, and riding her skateboard like them. The girls didn't like her because she was too boyish. She didn't have patience for talking about crushes or dresses or makeup like the rest of the girls she knew.

She buried her face in her arms and sank deeper into feeling sorry for herself. *I'm not pretty, either,* she thought. She felt that her blue eyes were too close together. Her sandy hair, normally tucked under a baseball cap, she saw as straight and stringy. She had freckles all over her nose. She'd just entered into a growth spurt that made her arms and legs go awkward lengths. They were too long for her body, she thought. Nobody wanted to be friends with someone like that, she concluded.

She was a misfit.

When Mark came to Odyssey, he was a misfit, too—that's why they became such good friends.

She clenched the letter in her fist and wondered if a good cry might help. Nobody in the world felt as lonely as she did at that moment; she was sure of it.

"Patti?" her mother called from beyond the bedroom door.

"Yeah, Mom?"

The door opened, and Susan Eldridge peered in. "What are you doing?"

"Reading Mark's letter," Patti replied as she sat up on her bed.

Mrs. Eldridge looked at the crumpled letter. "Isn't it hard to read like that?" she asked.

"There wasn't much to read," Patti said, then sighed.

"He didn't have much to say?" Mrs. Eldridge asked and smiled sympathetically.

"No, he says he's happy. Nice of him to let me know," Patti growled.

"Terrible, isn't it?" Mrs. Eldridge said as she sat down on the edge of the bed. She wrapped her hand around one of the canopy posts. "Imagine the nerve of him getting on with his life!"

"Don't tease me," Patti said.

Mrs. Eldridge rubbed Patti's leg softly. "I know how you feel. It doesn't seem fair that Mark should go back to Washington and be happy. He should be wasting away, miserable without your friendship."

"Yeah!" Patti exclaimed. "He should be. Why should he get to be happy when *I'm* not happy?"

"Is it really so bad for you?" Mrs. Eldridge asked, concerned.

Patti gazed at her mother and realized she was confessing something she hadn't told *anyone* up until now. "He's the only friend I ever had," she said. The words caught in her throat, and she fought back the tears that had threatened to come all morning. Patti's mom reached for her, but she suddenly leaped off the bed and prowled around the room. "I'm not going to cry," she said angrily. "I don't *care* if he's happy. I don't care *what* he does."

Mrs. Eldridge watched her daughter for a moment, then said, "Mark is doing the right thing if he's getting on with his life. You should do the same, Patti."

"How?" Patti challenged.

Mrs. Eldridge thought about it for a moment before replying, "That's a good question. Let's think it over and see what we can come up with."

"I didn't say I wanted to turn it into a homework assignment, Mom," Patti said.

"You'd rather sit around and mope?"

Patti shrugged. "I can't think of anything better to do."

Mrs. Eldridge smiled and stood up. "I can. Your father and I want to take you somewhere to forget your woes."

"Really?" Patti asked hesitantly. "Like where?"

"The spring carnival."

CHAPTER TWO

The spring carnival had been a tradition in Odyssey for as long as Patti could remember. It came every year to Brook Meadow—a large expanse of land just off the bypass to Connellsville—when the kids were on a week-long spring break from school. With a large Ferris wheel, salt-and-pepper shakers, merry-go-round, bumper cars, hall of mirrors, arcades, galleries, cotton candy, and stuffed-animal prizes, the carnival was a welcome relief to everyone after being shut in all winter. As a young girl, Patti had thought that spring wouldn't come to Odyssey unless the carnival arrived first.

"It's a shame this'll be the last one," Bob Eldridge said as he handed his daughter a box of popcorn at the carnival later that morning.

"What?" Patti asked, alarmed.

"It's not the last one, Bob," Mrs. Eldridge quickly corrected her husband. "It's just the last time the carnival will be held here at Brook Meadow."

"No. Don't say that," Patti said with a frown. "It's *always* been at Brook Meadow. That's where the carnival belongs. They can't do it anywhere else."

Mr. Eldridge dipped into Patti's box and withdrew a fistful of popcorn. "Sorry, but it's already settled," he said. "The government bought Brook Meadow to build some kind of office complex."

"Which government?" she asked, glancing up at the Ferris wheel, which seemed to roll and sparkle against the clear, blue sky.

"Hm?" Her father was preoccupied watching a man trying to knock down milk bottles with a softball. "The federal government, who else?" Mr. Eldridge finally answered.

Patti shook her head. She felt even more depressed at the thought of another change in her life. "I think we should write to the president. Don't they have enough office buildings in Washington? Tell him to leave Odyssey alone."

"I'll sign a petition if you get one started," Patti's father said playfully.

They moved away from the popcorn stand into the crowd. People seemed to crisscross in every direction in front of them; parents tugged at the hands of gesturing children, couples walked hand in hand, and teens pushed and laughed at each other. On the Whipper-Snapper, a group of girls screamed as their cab was flung from one end of the ride to the other. Patti took it all in but didn't feel as though their fun had anything to do with her. Her parents tried to coax her onto some of the rides, but she wasn't interested.

"How about the hall of mirrors?" Mrs. Eldridge asked. "You always liked that."

"No, thanks," Patti said.

"You really don't want to shake this mood of yours, do you?" Mr. Eldridge observed wryly.

Patti just shrugged.

He took Mrs. Eldridge's hand. "Well, we're going to have a good time whether you are or not. Let's go." He pulled at his wife's arm and led her toward the hall of mirrors.

"We'll catch up with you later," Mrs. Eldridge said just before they turned to go in.

Alone, Patti stood and ate popcorn, watching the people moving to and fro, the colorful banners and streamers floating gently in the cool breeze, and the rides spinning, twirling, and bobbing. Her eye caught one of the carnival barkers—a large, heavyset man in grease-stained overalls. He rubbed the stubble on his chin and smiled at her. Most of his teeth were missing. She winced and rushed in the opposite direction. His sudden burst of laughter trailed behind her.

The encounter made her aware of all the other ticket-takers, barkers, and mechanics who worked for the carnival. She thought she remembered them as clean-cut young men and women who were spotlessly dressed and polite. But the workers she saw today as she continued walking looked downright seedy. Cigarettes dangled from their twisted lips. Grease and oil smudged their clothes, faces, and hair. They seemed to either leer at their customers or ignore them completely.

Mr. Whittaker had always told her not to judge people by their outward appearances, but, with this crew, she couldn't help it. They made her nervous.

"Hi, Patti."

Startled, Patti jumped and cried out. She dropped her popcorn box. Fortunately, it was now empty.

Donna Barclay eyed her warily. "Are you all right?" she asked.

"Yeah. I didn't see you come up," Patti said. She grabbed the empty box, spied a trash can, and went to put the box in.

Donna said as she followed along, "You look like you're in a world of your own."

Patti nodded. "I'm waiting for my parents. They're in the hall of mirrors."

"My family's on the Ferris wheel," Donna explained. "I don't like heights."

"Oh," Patti said. She dropped the popcorn box in the trash and glanced awkwardly around. She didn't know where the hall of mirrors was anymore. She'd walked farther than she had thought.

"Are you going to the lock-in at Whit's End tonight?" Donna asked.

"I don't know. I might be busy."

"Really?" Donna was surprised.

Patti read her surprise the wrong way and snapped, "What's wrong? I have things to do, you know. I have a life away from Whit's End."

Donna held up her hands defensively. "Don't get mad," she said. "I just thought that all the kids were going. I was surprised that you might not."

"Well, I'm not sure," Patti said, turning red-faced for getting so annoyed so quickly. She softened her tone. "I'll have to think about it."

"Okay . . ." Donna waited a moment, and when it was clear there was nothing else to say, she shoved her hands into her jacket pockets and made as if to leave. "Then maybe I'll see you later," she said.

"Yeah, maybe."

Donna hesitated, then said, "Patti . . . y'know, maybe we should do something together sometime. I always see you around, but I don't really know you very well."

"Yeah, sure," Patti said doubtfully. She knew that Donna had her own group of friends, and they'd never let someone like Patti in.

Donna nodded as if they'd agreed on something, then walked away.

She feels sorry for me, Patti thought. *I don't want her sympathy.* She kicked at the dirt, tugged at her baseball cap, and walked on. She didn't know where she was going but simply wanted to get away from anyone she might know. She wished she hadn't come to the carnival. She wanted to go home now. Looking around to see if she could find the hall of mirrors again, she ducked around a ticket booth and nearly ran into another girl.

"Excuse me," they both said at the same time. It sounded like one voice. The girl didn't look at Patti, but Patti caught sight of her face before she strode away. It took a moment, but Patti suddenly realized that she and the girl looked a lot alike. It was shocking enough to make Patti turn to find the stranger, just to make sure she wasn't seeing things.

The girl was already several yards away at a cotton candy vendor. Patti watched her. *This is really weird,* she thought. It was like watching herself. The girl wore the same style of jeans, sneakers, and sweatshirt. She had the same shape of face and profile as Patti, including the tufts of brown hair that stuck out from under a baseball cap.

The resemblance was so strong that it took Patti's breath away. She could have been a long-lost sister. She wanted to call out to the girl, to talk to her and find out who she was, where she lived, and if they were anything alike. Maybe they were long-lost soul mates who were supposed to meet at this carnival and become friends. Patti had read novels where that happened. Why couldn't it happen in real life?

Patti took a step forward and raised her hand to her mouth as a megaphone so she could call out. Oblivious to Patti, however, the girl grabbed her cotton candy and suddenly disappeared into the crowd.

Patti's heart sank into a sad, lonely place. Everything seemed to conspire to keep her in a bad mood. She thought of Mark again and felt that urge to cry. Again she refused. It was one thing to feel sorry for herself; it was another to make a scene in the middle of a carnival. She wouldn't cry.

She made her way back in the direction of the bright, flashing lights advertising the hall of mirrors—or so she thought. After a moment, she realized she'd gone in the wrong direction and was somewhere on the outskirts of the carnival. The dazzling lights she'd seen were actually for a house of horrors. Grotesque monsters of wax lined the front of the makeshift trailer. A man dressed up as Count Dracula called out to the passersby to come in for the fright of their lives.

Next to the house of horrors, in a small clearing by itself, sat a green tent with faded gold lining and purple tassels over the entrance. A hand-painted sign rested against one of the tent pegs. "Madam Clara," it read. "Your Future Awaits Inside."

Patti looked at the entrance, then the sign, then the entrance again. Curiosity rose up within her. She'd heard of fortune-tellers and clairvoyants—people who could supposedly tell the future. The pastor at her church said that people who practiced such things were wrong and often against God. On the one or two occasions when her parents mentioned them, it was to call them frauds.

Patti wondered about it. Could someone know the future by reading your palm or looking at special kinds of cards? What was her future going to be like? She glanced around quickly to see if anyone she knew was nearby. She saw only a few strangers and stragglers. The crowds were in other parts of the carnival.

Would it be so wrong just to see who Madam Clara was and what she had to say? Patti didn't have to believe anything the woman said. But it would be nice to know if the days ahead were going to be as depressing as today had been.

Patti walked to the entrance of the tent and peered in. Inside, it was dark and barren except for a small table and two chairs in the middle of a dirt floor. A candle flickered on the center of the table. Patti's better sense told her it would be a mistake to go inside. She should go find her parents now.

"Come in, my dear," an old woman said, stepping out of the shadows at the rear of the tent.

"I think I'm at the wrong place," Patti stammered and retreated a step.

"Are you so sure?" The woman looked just like a gypsy from *The Hunchback of Notre Dame.* She had a scarf tied over her wild, white hair. Her blouse was striped and hung loose beneath a vest of black and gold. She wore a long, black skirt that made it look as if she drifted rather than walked across the ground. She smiled, and her face turned into a series of wrinkles, crow's-feet, and deep lines on deeply tanned skin.

"Yes, ma'am," Patti said quickly. "I was looking for the hall of mirrors."

The woman chuckled softly as if the statement had deep meaning for her. "I have never had my little tent confused with a hall of mirrors," she said, "though there are reflections here that might show people their true selves. But you are early."

Patti didn't understand a word she'd just heard. "Sorry, but—"

"Let me see your face, child," the woman said, and she opened the tent flap farther to let the sunlight in. She gazed at Patti, taking her in from head to foot. Patti thought the woman's expression had changed for a moment, as if she recognized her from somewhere. The old woman said quietly, almost as a secret, "You are in the right place, child. I am Madam Clara, the one you are to see. Come in."

"I made a mistake," Patti began to say, but the woman wasn't listening. She had sat down at the table and crossed her hands in front of her, as if waiting patiently for Patti to do the same. Patti considered running out. But the desire not to be rude mixed with her natural curiosity and led her to the table.

"That's right. Sit down." Madam Clara smiled.

Patti obeyed but said abruptly, "I don't believe in this stuff. I only came in because I—"

"The less you say, the better. I know why you are here, and it is my role to help you. It's all arranged."

"Arranged?"

The woman leaned forward and whispered, "We know, don't we? You have come to me, and I will help you. Don't be coy, child. Let us not play games. Now, say the words."

"The words?"

The woman nodded.

"What words?"

The woman smiled knowingly. "I see. You don't trust me. Of course, why should you? Here is a strange old woman who asks for your trust. You are wise not to give it until you have proof."

Patti was intrigued. If the woman gave proof of her

ability to tell the future, maybe the visit would be worthwhile. “What kind of proof?”

Madam Clara suddenly produced a deck of cards—from where, Patti couldn’t tell. The old woman quickly dealt out five of the cards and laid them face down on the table.

“My father does card tricks,” Patti said, unimpressed.

“Does he?” Madam Clara tapped the top of one of the cards. “This is no trick.” She turned the card over to reveal a queen of hearts. “This is your card,” she said.

“My card?”

“You are skeptical and want proof. This is your proof.”

Patti stared at the card as if it might suddenly do something magical. When it didn’t, she asked, “How does this prove anything?”

Madam Clara snatched up the card and thrust it at Patti. “Take this card to the shooting gallery and I promise you’ll win something special.”

Patti hesitantly took the card. “That’s my future? I’m going to win something at the shooting gallery?”

“You will indeed,” Madam Clara said as she stood up. “The very thing you want. I promise. And then you will believe. Now go. I will not see you again until you are convinced.”

Confused, Patti also stood up. “But what about—”

“No more words. Go, child,” Madam Clara said, then walked into the dark shadows at the rear of the tent.

Patti watched her go, looked at the queen of hearts, then strolled out into the sunlight.

CHAPTER THREE

Patti wandered around the carnival and looked for her parents. When she couldn't find them, she decided to visit the shooting gallery. Her encounter with Madam Clara was so bizarre that she couldn't resist seeing what would happen next.

The man in charge of the shooting gallery was a wiry fellow with thinning, blond hair, round, gold spectacles, and a large sweater that obscured most of his body and the upper half of his thin legs. "Step right up! Takes just a buck to try your best against the dancing ducks!" he barked.

The ducks truly did dance—mechanically along the back wall of the gallery. They suddenly appeared on the far left and rose up in Daffy-Duck-like twirls, moving up and down, backward and forward, before eventually disappearing on the far right. Hitting any one of them would be quite a trick, Patti thought. No wonder few people seemed interested in playing.

She eyed the prizes hanging by strings overhead. They

included small, cheesy-looking stuffed animals, coloring books, balloons, and one large stuffed bear. The bear—brown, furry, and maintaining a sad expression on its face—was by far the most appealing trophy to be won *if* Madam Clara's prediction was right. A sign pinned to its belly said, "Three in a row to go."

"Are you interested, little lady?" the man behind the counter asked.

"Well, I . . ." Patti wasn't sure what to say. She pulled the queen of hearts from her back pocket and laid it on the counter. "I'm supposed to give you this."

The man's eyes grew wide, then he picked up the card and handed it back to her. "A complimentary player," he said pleasantly. "Not sure what the ducks'll do when no bucks are involved. But grab your gun and see."

Shoving the card back into her pocket, Patti grabbed one of the rifles from the counter, lifted it to her shoulder, and took aim.

"Ready?" he asked.

Patti wasn't but said, "I guess."

He flipped a switch that momentarily stopped the mechanical ducks. A second later, they suddenly came to life. One after another, they emerged on the left, quacking through a loudspeaker as they moved. Patti fired the rifle just as one of the ducks lifted up. She was sure she missed. But she heard a loud "bing," and the duck lit up in a bright red color. "Got me," it quacked, then slipped away behind a marsh facade.

"Nice shot," the man said.

"Thanks," Patti said as she took aim and pulled the trigger. Direct hit. Again there was a loud "bing," and the next mechanical duck turned bright red with a loud "Got me!" It fell into the marsh facade just like the other one.

"You're pretty good," said the man.

Better than I ever thought, Patti mused. She took aim again and was just about to pull the trigger when a hand fell on her shoulder.

"There you are," her father said.

Patti turned to him and accidentally pulled the trigger. "Oops," she said. But instantly there was the telltale "bing," and another duck quacked "Got me!" in protest and disappeared into the marsh facade.

"Good shootin', Tex," Mr. Eldridge said with a laugh.

"I didn't know you were a hunter," Mrs. Eldridge added with a smile.

"How did I do that?" Patti asked. "There was no way I could've hit that duck."

"Hit it you did, little lady," the man behind the counter exclaimed as he reached up and grabbed the big bear.

Patti's jaw fell. "I won the bear?"

"Three in a row and he's yours to go," the man said. With a grunt, he hoisted the bear across the counter.

It took both of Patti's arms to carry him. "Thank you," she said happily.

"A prize for the queen of hearts," the man said with a smile.

His remark stopped Patti in her tracks. She had forgotten about Madam Clara and her prediction. What did this mean? Had the old woman really told Patti's future? Was she supposed to go back now to learn more?

"The queen of hearts?" Mr. Eldridge asked as they walked away.

Patti blushed and shrugged. She wasn't sure it'd be a good idea to tell her parents about Madam Clara or what had just happened. Mostly, she didn't want to get in trouble.

"Are you happy now?" asked Mrs. Eldridge.

"I have a new friend," Patti replied.

Mr. Eldridge put his arm around his daughter's waist and said, "On that pleasant note, maybe we should go home."

Patti sat the bear next to her on the backseat of the car and pondered over a name for him. As her father guided the car out of the makeshift parking lot on Brook Meadow, Patti glanced back toward the carnival. She felt strangely guilty for winning the bear and not returning to Madam Clara. But how could she without explaining it all to her mother and father?

Dust kicked up behind the car, and for an instant, Patti thought she saw her look-alike—the girl she had bumped into by the ticket booth. She nearly called out to her parents to look at the girl. But then the girl pointed in Patti's direction. The shooting-gallery man was suddenly at her side, squinting to see the Eldridges' car. They were joined by several other workers from the carnival. One boy even made as if to chase after the car, but Mr. Eldridge had already turned onto the main highway. Patti nervously squirmed in her seat to look out the back window. The small crowd faded into the distance.

Patti sank low in the seat and wondered what the fuss was about. Why were they all so agitated? Were they mad because she didn't go back to Madam Clara? Why would they care?

She looked quizzically at her new bear as if he might answer her silent questions. He stared back at her in silence.

CHAPTER FOUR

"I'm going to call him Binger," Patti announced to her parents when they got home. She pulled the big bear from the backseat.

"Why Binger?" her father asked.

"Because the ducks kept going 'bing' when I hit them."

"Oh. I thought it was because he looks like Bing Crosby," Mr. Eldridge said.

"Who?" Patti inquired.

"The one who sang 'White Christmas,'" Mrs. Eldridge said.

Patti took Binger up to her room and carefully positioned him on the chair to her small study desk. He watched her as she paced around the room, her face pressed into an expression of deep thought.

"Do you believe in fortune-telling?" Patti asked the bear. "I mean, is it possible that I really won you because Madam Clara predicted I would?"

The bear didn't reply.

Patti continued, "Maybe it was some kind of setup. But how? *Why?* Why would they go to all that trouble just to impress me?"

Binger refused to comment.

"Do you think I should tell my parents about it? It was really strange when that girl who looked like me pointed at us as we drove away. And then that guy from the shooting gallery showed up and that kid tried to chase us and . . ." Patti sat down on the edge of her bed. "Maybe I should've gone back to Madam Clara. I don't believe in all this telling-the-future stuff, but I won you, didn't I? Just like she said I would."

Binger tilted his head thoughtfully for a moment, then slumped completely to one side and fell off the chair. Patti scooped him up and hugged him close on her lap.

"I'm glad I won you," Patti said. "I don't care how it happened."

In another part of the house, the phone rang. One of Patti's parents must've picked it up, because it stopped after the second ring. A moment later, Mr. Eldridge called up the stairs for Patti.

"Yeah, Dad?" Patti called back.

"Mr. Whittaker is on the phone for you," he said.

"Mr. Whittaker wants to talk to me?" Patti was surprised. Mr. Whittaker—or *Whit,* as he was often called by other adults—was the owner of Whit's End, a popular soda shop and renowned "discovery emporium" filled with room after room of interactive displays, games, activities, books, and all-around fun for kids.

"I think he wants to personally invite you to the lock-in tonight," Mr. Eldridge explained. "He talked your mother and I into being chaperones. Take it on the extension."

Patti was impressed: It was a big deal to get a call from someone as important as Mr. Whittaker. Still clutching Binger, she crossed the hall to her parents' room. The phone was on the nightstand next to their bed. She picked up the receiver and said, "Hello?"

"Hi, Patti," Whit said in a deep, friendly voice. Patti could instantly imagine his round face with its large, white mustache and matching crown of wild, bushy, white hair. "I just spoke to your parents about the lock-in at Whit's End tonight."

"That's what Dad said."

"I guess you know that they'll help chaperone. But they agreed only if I can persuade you to come, too. Will you do us the honor?"

Patti hadn't thought about the lock-in since her encounter with Donna Barclay. She hesitated. "Uh, well . . ."

"We haven't seen you at Whit's End much over the past few months," he went on. "Frankly, I miss you. It'd be good to see you again . . . unless you've already made other plans."

Patti couldn't pretend that she had anything else to do. "Yeah—I mean, no—I don't have any other plans."

"So you'll come tonight?"

"Yeah, I guess so."

"Good. We'll see you later."

"Okay." She hung up the phone and only then realized that her mother was standing in the doorway to the bedroom.

"I think you'll enjoy yourself," Mrs. Eldridge said. "You never know what'll happen when you're at Whit's End."

Patti nodded. It was true. Whit's End was the most unpredictable place she'd ever known. But she'd shied away from it over the past few months. She felt as though she didn't have any reason for going anymore. It wasn't as if she had any friends there, apart from Mr. Whittaker. But he was a grown-up, so that didn't seem to count.

"You can even take Binger with you," her mother added.

****

"Now I'll finally get to see what happens at a lock-in," Mr. Eldridge said as they loaded the car with sleeping bags, boxes of potato chips, and some cakes and pies Mrs. Eldridge had spent the rest of the afternoon making.

Mrs. Eldridge carefully placed another pie on the backseat. "Our church used to have lock-ins when I was growing up," she said. "I wonder if they're the same?"

"Probably," Patti said. "We stay up all night and play a lot of games, eat tons of food, have a Bible study and sometimes a trivia contest, and try to keep each other awake for as long as possible." She pushed Binger across the backseat until he was pressed against the various boxes of goodies. "No sampling the food until later," she warned him.

They arrived at Whit's End just as the sun was going down. Silhouetted against the darkening sky, the old Victorian building looked like a hodgepodge collection of square boxes, sharp angles, and rounded edges. Patti had learned from Mr. Whittaker some of the history of his shop. The tower, for example, was once part of a church. Another section had been used as the city's recreation center. And there was a maze of tunnels underneath that were used by runaway slaves in the days of the Underground Railroad. Mr. Whittaker had also added and changed parts of the building to suit his own needs, putting in a small theater for plays and musicals, a library for the kids to do their homework in, and one room that contained the county's largest train set. Patti knew that Mr. Whittaker would let the kids use all the rooms during the lock-in—and there would be no end to the fun.

Why didn't I want to come? she asked herself.

A couple of girls from school passed by just as Patti pulled Binger from the backseat. "Aw, look," one of them said, "she brought her teddy bear to sleep with."

The girls giggled and walked away.

Patti blushed self-consciously.

Mr. Eldridge was suddenly at Patti's side. He scrubbed his clean-shaven chin and peered through his glasses at her thoughtfully. "You know, sweetheart, maybe we should leave Binger in the car," he said. "It might look like you're showing off if you take him inside. Few of the kids own such an impressive bear."

Patti looked at her father gratefully. She knew he was giving her a way out of her embarrassment. "Good idea," she said.

"Most bears are still hibernating now anyway," he added as he grabbed Binger by the arms. "I'll put him in the trunk where it'll be dark and comfortable, the way bears like it."

Patti smiled at her dad, even though she felt as if she'd suddenly turned back into a five-year-old. *Am I really acting so childish?* she wondered. She thought back to her reaction to Mark Prescott's letter and how she had pouted at the carnival, even doing something as silly as going to a fortune-teller. *Yes,* she concluded, *I'm acting like a baby.* She decided that this lock-in would be the perfect place to start acting her age.

Inside Whit's End, Patti was surprised to find that Mr. Whittaker had set up even more activities than she'd imagined. Tom Riley, Mr. Whittaker's best friend, was sponsoring a table tennis tournament in the Little Theater. Connie Kendall, a teenager whom Mr. Whittaker had hired just a couple of months before, was pulling together volunteers for the water-balloon races. Mr. Whittaker was recruiting contestants for the Bible contest. In some ways, it reminded Patti of the carnival.

At first glance, she figured more than 30 kids were there for the lock-in—and that didn't count the ones who were in other parts of the building. Many of them she recognized. Jack Davis, Matt Booker, and Oscar Peterson were arguing over whether they should play table tennis first or go upstairs to the train set. Robyn Jacobs and her sister, Melanie, were in one of the booths, finishing ice cream sodas. Karen Crosby, Donna Barclay, and Lucy Cunningham-Schultz stood in front of a display of paintings Mr. Whittaker had set up and seemed lost in conversation about one of them.

Everyone seemed to be with friends—*close* friends. Patti felt her heart sink a little. That's why she'd been so moody after Mark's letter; it reminded her of how alone she was.

"You came!" Donna Barclay exclaimed as she walked over from Karen and Lucy.

Patti shrugged. "My parents decided to help chaperone," she said, "and I thought I might as well come along."

"Good," Donna said. "I think this is going to be a lot of fun. My parents are chaperoning, too. They're upstairs helping with the Around-the-World game."

"Around the World?"

"Mr. Whittaker set up one of the rooms with displays of various places around the world. You have to guess where they are." She suddenly giggled and said, "I'm hoping my brother will get lost in the Amazon or get stuck on the North Pole."

"Jimmy's here, too?"

"Everybody's here," Donna said. "I'm glad you came."

Patti eyed Donna carefully. It didn't make sense that she would be so friendly. Did she want something?

"What are you going to do first?" Donna asked as if she didn't notice Patti's silence.

Patti looked around. "I think I'll join the table tennis tournament."

"That's what all the boys are doing," Donna said, rolling her eyes.

"Then it's probably time for some of the girls to show them how to play the game," Patti said defiantly. She walked over to Tom Riley's sign-up table, grabbed a pen, and added her name to the list.

"Good for you, Patti," Tom said with a smile.

No sooner had she finished than she was aware of Donna at her elbow.

"You're right," Donna said. "It's time to show the boys what's what." She scribbled her name at the bottom of the sheet. Then she grabbed Patti's arm. "Come look at this painting Mr. Whittaker brought in from the Odyssey Museum. Karen and Lucy and I were trying to figure out if it's a boat, a large banana, or a really small lake."

****

The night spun away in a frenzy of activities. Patti not only made it to the finals of the table tennis tournament (she was eventually beaten by Mike Henderson), but she also finished first in the water-balloon race and was the first to identify Mr. Whittaker's display for Sri Lanka in the Around-the-World Game (she'd had to do a report about Sri Lanka for Mrs. Walker's history class last year).

She never had a minute alone to feel sorry for herself. Donna Barclay was always nearby to make sure she stayed involved. Patti didn't mind. The better she got to know Donna, the more she saw how much they had in common. Though Donna wasn't a tomboy like Patti, she was interested in different kinds of sports, and they shared a mutual hatred of algebra. For that reason, Patti agreed to go to Donna's house the next day to work on some math homework together.

It was well past midnight when Mr. Whittaker served up a light snack for the kids, who were beginning to get sleepy. A few had already curled up in their sleeping bags and drifted off in the corners.

To stay awake, Patti volunteered to help clear the dishes. She carried a tray to the kitchen, where Connie Kendall was already hard at work with the jet spray. Connie was a teenager in high school (Patti didn't know what grade). She stood just a little taller than Patti and had straight, black hair, a slender, pleasant face, and an energetic manner that livened up her facial expressions and hand gestures. "She's a ball of fire, all right," she heard Tom Riley say at one point in the evening.

"I don't think we've met," Connie said and thrust a soap-covered hand at Patti. "I'm Connie Kendall."

Patti shook her wet hand, then dumped the tray of dishes into the large sink. "I'm Patti."

"I know," Connie replied. "You're the one Whit is so worried about."

"I am?"

Connie frowned, her bright eyes clouding for a moment. "Oh, I don't think I was supposed to say that. Sorry. It's just that he's been talking about you the past couple of days. It was really important to him that you come to the lock-in. He said you had a close friend who moved away last summer and you've had a hard time coping with the change."

"Mr. Whittaker said all that?" Patti was surprised. She'd had no idea that Mr. Whittaker was paying so much attention to her. It made her wonder if asking her parents to chaperone was part of the plan to get her to Whit's End. Maybe Donna was part of the scheme, too.

"Mark, right? Your friend's name was Mark," Connie continued. With the back of her hand, she pushed a stray lock of hair away from her forehead. "See, I think Whit mentioned it all to me because he knows I've been having a hard time adjusting to living in Odyssey. I moved here from California because my mom and dad got a divorce, and, well, Odyssey's a small town compared to Los Angeles. Do you know what I mean?"

Patti explained, "I've lived in Odyssey most of my life, so it's hard for me to compare it to anywhere else."

"If you lived in Los Angeles, you'd know what I'm talking about. We had everything there—right around the corner. Good movie theaters and gigantic malls and every kind of store you can imagine." Connie rinsed off a couple of plates and sighed heavily. "I want to go back as soon as I can."

Patti opened her mouth to say something about her own feelings, about being lonely for a close friend like Mark, but Connie didn't give her a chance.

Connie continued, "I'm saving up for a bus ticket—or maybe I'll find a cheap plane fare. I'll go by boat if I have to.

It's been really tough. My mom is happy here, I think. She has relatives in the area. My Uncle Joe, for one. Actually, he's *her* Uncle Joe, but I call him Uncle Joe, too, because it sounds goofy to call him my *Great-Uncle Joe*. Do you want to take that bag of trash out back to the Dumpster?"

Patti almost missed Connie's question. "What?" she said.

"The trash," Connie said more slowly. "Do you want to take it out to the Dumpster?"

"Sure," Patti replied, then grabbed the large, green bag. It was heavier than it looked, and she had to use both hands to carry it through the back door and over to the large, brown trash container along the side of the shop. It was dark outside. The moon had disappeared behind a thick cloud covering. The yellow porch light flickered unevenly as if the bulb might go out at any minute. Patti put the bag down so she could slide the Dumpster's door open. She had just reached for the handle when a hand fell on her shoulder.

Patti cried out as she spun around, stumbled on the trash bag, and fell backward against the Dumpster.

Madam Clara stood over her and said with a crooked smile, "Hello, child."

CHAPTER FIVE

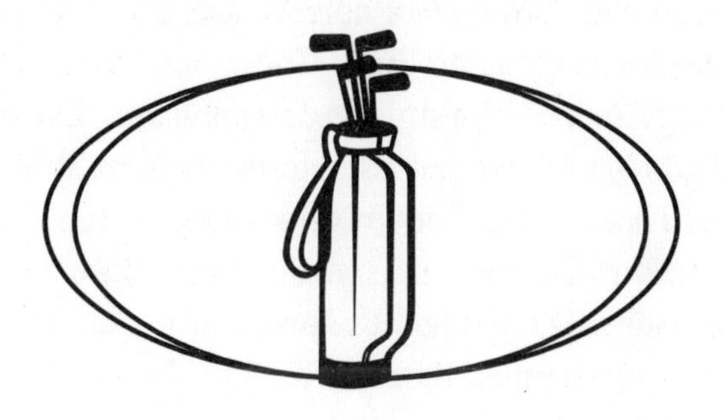

"Madam Clara!" Patti gasped.

"I've frightened you. I'm so sorry," the old woman said and helped Patti to her feet. Her hands felt like leather.

Patti glanced toward the back door nervously. "What are you doing here?" she asked.

"Seeking you out. I have had a premonition—"

"A what?"

"Call it a vision of your future," Madam Clara explained, then held her hand up as if she were making a vow. "Tonight, the cards made it clear that you are not safe. That is why I came to find you."

"How did you know I was here?" Patti asked.

"The cards tell me everything."

"The cards," Patti said warily.

Madam Clara frowned. "You are still skeptical."

"You have to admit, it's a little hard to believe—"

"It is not hard for those who *choose* to believe!" Madam Clara exclaimed. "Was I not correct when I said you would win at the shooting gallery?"

"Yes . . ." Patti admitted. "But that might have been a trick."

Madam Clara threw her hands into the air. "Why would I trick you? I have not asked you for money. I have asked for nothing. I expected only that you would return to me after you won your prize and had the proof of my ability that you had sought. Was that so much to ask?"

"No." Patti hung her head guiltily.

Madam Clara touched Patti's arm gently and said in an understanding voice, "You were afraid to come back, I know. Perhaps you didn't want anyone to know that we had spoken. You haven't told anyone, have you?"

Patti shook her head. "No," she answered. "Actually, my parents would be mad if they found out."

"Then do not tell your parents," Madam Clara said. "Tell no one at all. What I must say is for your ears only."

"Why?"

The old woman leaned closer to Patti. "I have said it already. You are not safe. The cards have told me that you are in danger."

"What kind of danger?" asked Patti, still unsure of whether to believe the woman.

"The hearts on the cards," Madam Clara said as if that answered her question. "I have seen them. They spell trouble for you. Things will happen if we do not—"

Suddenly, the back door squeaked as Connie opened it.

"Patti," she said, "were you calling me?" She squinted into the darkness toward the Dumpster.

"No, Connie," Patti called back. "I was just talking to . . ." Gesturing toward Madam Clara, Patti turned. But Madam Clara was gone.

Connie took a few steps closer. "To who?" she asked. "Was somebody out here?"

Patti looked around. There was no sign that the old woman had ever been there. "I thought . . . I mean . . ." She didn't know what to say. "Maybe I'm more tired than I thought."

****

Patti was bothered by her bizarre meeting with Madam Clara. Had the old woman really come to warn her? What kind of trouble would she be in—except the trouble her parents would give her if they found out she'd spoken to a fortune-teller? Madam Clara had used the word *danger.* Why would Patti be in danger? Maybe it was some kind of trick. But why? Why would Madam Clara or anyone at the carnival play a prank on her?

Patti wrestled with these questions while she joined Mr. Whittaker and some of the kids in a middle-of-the-night game of Whit's Golf. The game, created by Mr. Whittaker, involved using large, plastic golf clubs to hit a round sponge-ball from room to room. Each room had a large can that served as a "hole" to hit the ball into. The angles and placement of the holes got more difficult with each room. As an added challenge, each hole also had a question about the Bible that the contestants had to answer for bonus points.

While playing, Patti toyed with the idea of talking to Mr. Whittaker about Madam Clara. He'd probably know what was going on—or be able to make a good guess. The only problem was that Mr. Whittaker would insist that Patti tell her parents about it. She wasn't ready to do that. Not yet.

The questions persisted. How had Madam Clara known Patti was at Whit's End? Had the cards really told her? Was it possible that Madam Clara really did have supernatural powers? Could she tell the future with cards and visions? She had predicted that Patti would win the bear. And, since that came true, maybe Patti really was in some kind of danger. But what kind—and why?

It was almost 3:00 in the morning when Patti and the other players got to the sixteenth hole in the golf game. Mr. Whittaker had just asked Bruce Neilson a question from the book of Deuteronomy when Connie appeared in the doorway to the library with a worried expression on her face.

"Whit," she said and gestured quickly.

Mr. Whittaker excused himself and walked over to Connie. All ears in the room strained to hear what she had to say as she whispered in an urgent tone. Only bits and pieces were loud enough to pick up. Patti heard enough to learn that Connie had seen someone outside, wandering around the building.

"At this time of night?" Mr. Whittaker said.

Connie nodded.

"You keep this game going while I check it out," Mr. Whittaker told Connie, then slipped out of the room.

Karen Crosby asked Connie, "There's someone sneaking around outside?"

"Maybe," Connie replied. "I saw someone out there, but it's probably nothing to worry about." Her face betrayed her feelings as her eyes kept darting to the doorway. She obviously wanted to go out and see what was happening.

Patti's knees suddenly felt strangely weak. If anyone was out there, it was probably Madam Clara. And if Mr. Whittaker caught her, Patti would have to explain, and Madam Clara's prediction would come true: Patti would be in *big* trouble.

Connie was just about to reread the question from Deuteronomy when they all heard the small bell above the front door jingle. Mr. Whittaker called out, "All right, what do you want?"

It was like an invitation for Patti, Connie, and the other kids to race from the library into the main soda shop area. Patti's heart galloped as she rounded the corner and saw Mr. Whittaker at the front door, talking to someone. As she got closer, she saw that the mysterious stranger was a man dressed in a dark suit. She breathed deeply with relief.

She crowded in with the kids closer to the door, only to realize that her relief was premature. On the other side of the man stood Madam Clara. Her eyes were alight with anger, and she scanned the faces of the gathering kids as if looking for someone.

"I'm Detective Anderson," the man said as he flashed his

badge at Mr. Whittaker. "I was driving past on my way home when I saw all the lights on. They had told me at the station that you were having a lock-in, but I'd forgotten. Then I saw a shadow move across the front porch and caught this woman. She won't answer any of my questions. I assume she's not connected to anyone here?"

Mr. Whittaker turned to Madam Clara. "Are you connected to anyone here, ma'am?" he asked. "Is there a reason you're on my porch?"

Madam Clara's jaw was set. She didn't answer but continued to look at the faces of the kids inside the door. Patti stepped a little behind Mike Henderson, who was bigger than she was, so she wouldn't be seen. Out of the corner of her eye, she saw her parents come down the stairs and cross toward the group at the door.

Mr. Whittaker then asked the crowd, "Does anyone know this woman?"

Patti's heart jumped. Mike moved, and Madam Clara suddenly made eye contact with her. The recognition was instant. "She knows me," Madam Clara said and pointed at Patti.

Everyone turned to Patti.

Hot blood surged through her veins. She felt herself turn red. Her eyes burned.

"Patti?" Mr. Whittaker prompted.

Patti struggled beneath the questioning eyes of her friends and the knowledge that her parents were nearby. Madam Clara locked her in a steely gaze. If she said yes, she'd have a lot of explaining to do. If she said no, then . . .

what? She swallowed hard and felt the panic rise within her. The split second that had passed since Mr. Whittaker's question seemed like an hour.

"No," Patti said, "I don't know her."

A buzz—like whispering bees—worked its way through the crowd. Madam Clara's eyes went wide with indignation.

"Let's go," the detective said to Madam Clara. "You can talk to me at the station."

"She's lying!" Madam Clara exclaimed in a loud, shaky voice.

The detective put a hand on her arm and said, "Yeah, right. Tell it to me at the station."

"You do not heed me!" Madam Clara wrenched free from the detective and lunged toward Patti. The kids shrieked and scattered, leaving Patti frozen in her place. Mr. Whittaker and the detective quickly grabbed the woman by the arms and held her back. She strained against them and shouted, "You have betrayed me! You do not believe—and your lack of belief will be a curse to you! Do you hear me? A curse!"

"That's enough," the detective said as he tugged at Madam Clara, drawing her away from the door and toward the front steps.

"A curse!" Madam Clara cried again as the detective led her away.

Patti was aware that everyone was looking at her. She sensed her parents moving from the other side of the crowd. Mr. Eldridge touched her arm. "Patti," he said.

She dissolved into tears.

CHAPTER SIX

Patti didn't remember much about the rest of the night. Her parents assumed that she'd cried because of the shock she'd gotten from Madam Clara. The kids turned Patti into an instant celebrity because she'd been singled out by "that crazy lady" (as they called her). And the less Patti wanted to talk about it—for fear that she might slip and prove she had lied—the more everyone was convinced that she had been deeply frightened by the experience.

Mr. Whittaker used the incident to talk to the kids about being very careful with strangers. Patti barely heard a word he said. Her mind was racing with the meaning of what had happened. Her stomach was in knots as she wondered what would happen next.

It occurred to her to tell her parents everything: just spill the beans about Madam Clara and the carnival. But the more she considered it, the less she liked the idea. She'd get in trouble on all sides—for going to a fortune-teller in the first place, and then for lying about it. *What a mess!* she thought.

Then there was the whole business of Madam Clara's curse. Did she really have that kind of power? Did *anyone?*

Mr. Whittaker addressed the kids on the subject as they all had breakfast together. "The Bible makes it clear that there are two kinds of supernatural forces at work in our world—God's and Satan's," he explained. "God is the most powerful. But Satan gets his tricks in, too. He's the great deceiver and will use lots of means to keep us distracted from God."

"You're going to have to explain that, Whit," Tom Riley said through a mouthful of cereal.

Mr. Whittaker smiled. "Okay, let's consider so-called curses. Can one human being put a curse on another? I'm doubtful. Few, if any, people have truly supernatural powers. Most of the time, people like that are merely using our own superstitions against us. What's the result? We spend our time worrying about Satan and what's he's up to rather than thinking about God and what *He's* trying to do. Satan just loves to keep us confused and distracted."

Connie leaned over to Patti and asked, "Do you believe in stuff like curses and bad luck?"

Patti shrugged.

"I do." Connie nodded toward Mr. Whittaker, who was still talking, and whispered, "Don't get me wrong. I think Whit is really smart, but I don't think he understands how the real world works. There are things we don't know about, like ESP and aliens from outer space and voodoo and horoscopes. Whit doesn't believe in them because they're not in the Bible."

"Don't you believe in the Bible?" Patti asked, surprised.

"Who, me?" Connie folded her arms and looked thoughtful for a moment. "I guess it's a good book. I haven't read it much. It's okay. But I don't think it has the last word about everything, if that's what you mean. For example, I was looking at my horoscope yesterday, and—"

"Is there something you want to say to us?" Mr. Whittaker asked Connie.

Connie sat up, blushed, and said, "Uh, no. I was just talking to Patti."

Mr. Whittaker nodded. "So I noticed. Patti, I hope you won't let what happened last night bother you. There's nothing to be afraid of."

"I know," Patti said, but she didn't believe it. It was easy to dismiss curses and bad luck when they happened to somebody else. But now she worried that something was going to happen to *her.*

After breakfast, the Eldridges wearily drove home.

"Patti," Mrs. Eldridge said along the way, "something's bothering you."

Patti squirmed on the backseat. "What do you mean?" she said.

"You recognized that woman, didn't you?"

"I saw her at the carnival," Patti said quickly. "But I don't *know* her."

"So you have no idea why she came to Whit's End?" her father asked.

Patti said truthfully, "No, it doesn't make any sense to me."

"Then I wonder why she got so upset with you?" Mrs. Eldridge said. "It's not every day you run into someone who decides to curse you."

Patti didn't have anything else to say. She stared out the window at the passing houses and the townsfolk getting up, starting their Saturday mornings. It all looked so normal. But Patti felt anything *but* normal. She felt as if she'd gotten herself into something bad. Worse, she had no idea what it was.

Once again, she thought about telling her parents the whole truth. Her conscience nagged at her the rest of the ride home, up the driveway, and into the garage. But she rationalized all the reasons it would be better not to.

"Let's unpack the car later," Mr. Eldridge said as they got out. "I'm too old for staying up all night. I need a nap."

Patti's mom agreed, and Patti was pleased that she wouldn't have to think or talk about Madam Clara again. In her heart, she wished the woman and her curses would simply disappear.

They stepped from the garage into the house, through the laundry room, into the kitchen, and through to the living room, where Patti's father suddenly stopped.

"Oh no!" he said.

Patti's mother gasped.

Patti peered around them and saw what they saw. It looked as if a tornado had gone through the place. Furniture was tossed over, books and keepsakes were swept from their shelves, and cabinet drawers were pulled out, their contents thrown carelessly on the floor.

"We've been robbed," Mr. Eldridge said, and he reached for the phone to call the police.

CHAPTER SEVEN

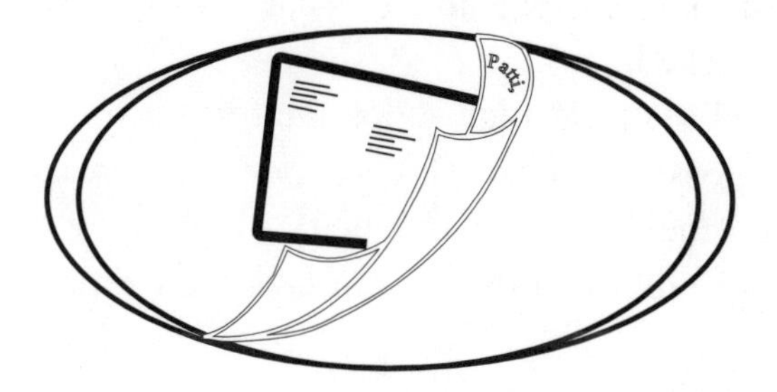

It's the curse. It's started already, Patti thought as she helped her mother clean up the living room. A couple of policemen had already searched the room for clues, dusted it for fingerprints, and moved into other parts of the house. Every room had been treated the same by the burglars. It looked as if they'd turned each one upside down. Detective Anderson, the same detective who'd caught Madam Clara the night before, was in charge of the investigation.

"They sure did a number on your place," Detective Anderson said as he surveyed the damage.

"The strange thing is that nothing seems to be missing," Mr. Eldridge observed.

"Nothing at all?" the detective asked. "Then they must have been looking for something. Do you keep anything valuable here—like jewelry, negotiable bonds, large amounts of cash?"

Mrs. Eldridge held up a broken statuette. "Nothing like

that," she said. "Most of what we own has only sentimental value." She added sadly, "This belonged to my grandmother."

"Anything else they might want from you?" Detective Anderson asked.

Mr. and Mrs. Eldridge shook their heads.

"It's possible they weren't looking for anything in particular," the detective continued. "Maybe they knew you'd be gone all night and decided to take their time tearing the place apart."

Mr. Eldridge scratched at his chin. "How could they know we'd be gone all night?" he asked. "We didn't know ourselves until a couple of hours before the lock-in."

The detective shrugged. "Maybe they've been watching your place for a while. Have you seen any strange vehicles or unusual people around?"

Patti's parents looked at each other, then to Patti. They all said no.

"The only stranger we've encountered is that woman you nabbed last night," Mr. Eldridge said. "What about her? Is it possible she's connected to this somehow?"

The detective slid his hands into his coat pockets and leaned against the wall. "It's possible, but not in a way I could prove."

"Didn't you question her last night?" asked Mrs. Eldridge.

"Sure," the detective answered. "But she was tight-lipped. She didn't say much at all. I had to let her go."

Surprised, Mr. Eldridge said, "You didn't arrest her?"

The detective smiled patiently. "You can hardly arrest

someone for walking on the porch at Whit's End, even at three in the morning. She was suspicious but did nothing criminal."

"My daughter remembered seeing the woman at the carnival yesterday," Patti's mother offered.

Detective Anderson nodded. "That's ultimately where I dropped her off. She's a fortune-teller there. Calls herself Madam Clara."

"She's a fortune-teller?" Mrs. Eldridge exclaimed, then shot a questioning glance at Patti. "Did you know that?"

Patti stared at her mother for a moment. The burden of her lies weighed heavily on her. She had no doubt that somehow the vandalism of their house was connected to Madam Clara's curse. And the curse was her fault. She didn't know how or why, but she knew it was.

"Yes," Patti said, choking on the word as the tears welled up in her eyes.

"Why didn't you say so?" her father asked.

Patti just shook her head.

"Is there anything else you haven't told us?" the detective inquired in a diplomatic voice.

Patti crumbled. It didn't matter how much trouble she got into, she decided, she had to tell them the truth. "Well, there is . . ." she said. And starting with her visit to Madam Clara's tent at the carnival, she proceeded to tell them everything that had happened, including winning Binger at the shooting gallery and her lie at Whit's End the night before. She hung her head in shame when she finished.

"I'm very disappointed in you," Mr. Eldridge said firmly. "You know better."

Patti agreed.

He went on: "I'm especially concerned that you think this fortune-teller has powers like that. Haven't we taught you what the Bible says? The woman is obviously a fraud."

"But how did she know I would win at the shooting gallery?" Patti asked.

"If I may interject," Detective Anderson said, "we see this all the time. The card she gave you—the one she said to show to the shooting-gallery barker—was a signal. When he saw the queen of hearts in your hand, he knew to rig the gallery so you'd win. They probably thought you'd be so impressed that you'd go back to her and pay to have your fortune told. Or, better still, you'd take your family and friends back. By winning the bear, you became a walking advertisement for the fortune-teller *and* the shooting gallery."

"That makes sense," Mr. Eldridge said. "But you *didn't* go back. It probably upset her."

"Did it upset her so much that she'd follow me to Whit's End?" Patti asked doubtfully.

The detective answered, "Maybe she wanted the bear back. Their scam backfired, and she got in trouble with the shooting-gallery barker. Who knows? It's also possible that she was a scout for whoever ransacked your house. She was sent there to make sure you didn't leave early to go home."

"Can you arrest her for that?" Mrs. Eldridge asked.

"No. We can't prove anything. It's all circumstantial. It

might even be nothing more than a coincidence."

"A coincidence!" Mrs. Eldridge cried out.

"I have to consider everything. But don't worry, I'll certainly question Madam Clara again," Detective Anderson said.

"It's amazing," Mr. Eldridge said. "All this fuss over a fortune-teller."

The detective nodded. "I've been suspicious of everyone who works at that carnival. They're a mangy-looking group. I've got some of my men keeping an eye on them." He gestured to Patti. "By the way—that prize you won. The bear."

"Binger?"

"Where is it now?"

Patti had to think for a minute. Did she leave him at Whit's End?

"He's in the trunk of the car," Mr. Eldridge said.

"I was thinking that I should take him with me," the detective offered. "He might be useful as evidence."

"Evidence? Evidence of what?" Mrs. Eldridge asked.

Patti was upset. "You can't take Binger! He's the only friend I have right now."

The detective held up his hands defensively. "Okay, it was a bad idea. Don't worry. It was just a thought. If he was what they were looking for, he'd be safer with me."

"But why would they go to all this trouble to get a stuffed bear back?" Mr. Eldridge wondered aloud.

"Beats me," the detective said. "I'm just toying with different theories. Forget I mentioned it."

Back in her room, Patti sat down on the edge of her bed. She had a big mess to clean up. All her dresser drawers had been emptied. Everything was pulled out of her closet, the clothes yanked from their hangers. She still couldn't escape the feeling that this was connected to Madam Clara's curse.

Her mother walked in, looked over the damage with a pained expression, then leaned against the doorway. "You know that your father and I can't just let what you did slide," she said. "Not only did you visit a fortune-teller—which you knew we wouldn't approve of—but then you kept it from us. And then you lied about knowing Madam Clara. You dug yourself in pretty deep."

"I'm sorry," Patti said. "It's like the whole thing spun out of control. It kept getting worse and worse until I was sure you two would hate me."

"We'd never hate you—not for anything you'd ever do! But that doesn't mean we have to like it when you do something wrong. You'll have to be disciplined. We'll start by making you clean up your room." She paused for a moment and then continued, "You know, Patti, this might not have happened if you hadn't felt so sorry for yourself earlier. Your life isn't so bad. And I think you saw last night that there are kids who want to be your friend. You just have to let them."

Patti agreed, then said jokingly, "It's all Mark's fault for sending me that letter." She glanced around the disaster area for Mark's letter. She'd left it on top of the desk, which didn't look as if it had been terribly disturbed by the vandals. "Where is it?" she asked after a minute of searching.

"Where's what?"

"Mark's letter. I left it on top of the desk."

"It's probably in the mess on the floor, which is as good a place to start to clean as any."

Patti took the hint and began reassembling her room. Three hours later, she had everything back where it belonged. Some of her keepsakes had been broken and couldn't be fixed. Sadly, she threw them away.

When she was finished, she sat back down on her bed. Her room looked almost as if nothing bad had happened. But she couldn't shake the feeling that her home had been invaded. Did it really have something to do with Madam Clara and her curse, or was it just a coincidence as Detective Anderson said? It was puzzling, too, that nothing seemed to be missing.

Patti suddenly remembered that in all the cleaning up, she hadn't found Mark's letter. Where could it be?

She yawned as a wave of sleepiness hit her. She hadn't slept at Whit's End, and it was beginning to catch up with her. A quick nap would be a good idea, she figured. She rolled onto her stomach, dropped her head onto the pillow, and pushed her hands underneath it. Her fingers brushed against something that felt like smooth paper.

She thought *Mark's letter* and grabbed the object. Pulling it out, she saw immediately that it wasn't the letter from Mark. It was a playing card: the jack of hearts.

CHAPTER EIGHT

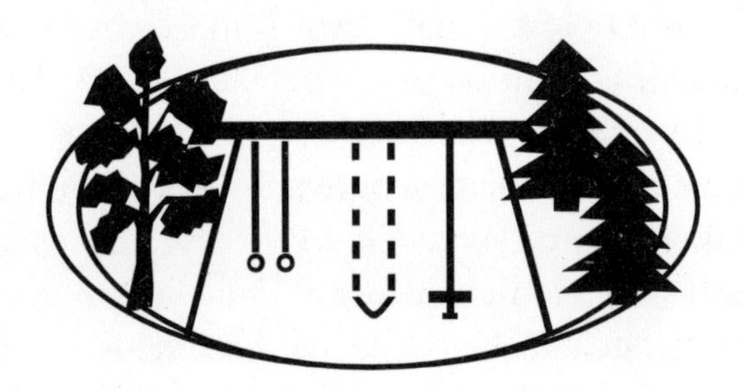

"This is remarkable," Detective Anderson said.

Patti's father had called him as soon as she had found the jack of hearts and told her parents. Careful not to smudge any fingerprints, Mr. Eldridge had picked the card up with a pair of tweezers and dropped it into a sandwich bag. It was something he'd seen once in the movies.

"Are you sure it's not from one of your decks?" the officer asked.

Patti replied from her place next to her mother and father on the living room couch, "We don't own any cards."

"Even if I did, I wouldn't own them with this design," Mrs. Eldridge added. She was referring to the intricate curls and flowers printed on the back of the card.

Detective Anderson compared it to the design on the back of the queen of hearts that Madam Clara had given Patti at the carnival. It was different. "It doesn't match," he observed.

"That's too bad," Mr. Eldridge said. "If it did, we'd have

proof that Madam Clara's behind this for some reason."

"But why?" Patti asked, echoing the question that had been nagging her ever since they came home to find the house ransacked. "Why would someone leave me that card?"

"I can't even begin to guess," the detective said. The easy chair squeaked as he leaned forward. "Didn't you say that Madam Clara warned you about the heart cards?"

"Yeah, but I didn't understand what she meant. Then Connie came out and she ran away," Patti said.

"Puzzling," the detective said as he looked again at the cards.

Mr. Eldridge pushed his glasses back up to the top of his nose and said, "What about Mark's letter? Why would they take it?"

"You're positive it isn't in your room?" Detective Anderson asked. "You didn't shove it in with your school papers?"

Patti shook her head. "I'm positive. I crunched it up a little, but then I either left it on my bed or my desk."

"It makes no sense to me. Why would they want a personal letter?" the detective mused. Then he said, "By the way, I questioned a few of the people at the carnival. They weren't helpful. Not only did they rudely refuse to answer most of my questions, but they also all had alibis for where they were while your house was broken into. Of course, they all vouched for each other."

Mr. Eldridge asked, "What about Madam Clara?"

"She denies that she went to Whit's End to see Patti."

"What?" Patti shouted in disbelief.

"Even after that overdramatic curse business?" Mrs. Eldridge asked.

The detective shrugged. "She said it was all for show. She was playing to the crowd to get them interested in coming to the carnival."

"No way." Patti folded her arms and frowned. What was Madam Clara up to?

"Did she explain why she was hanging around Whit's End at all?" Mrs. Eldridge asked.

"She said she'd gotten lost while searching for a convenience store to buy some medicine. She saw the lights at Whit's End and thought it was some kind of grocery store."

"That's absurd," Mr. Eldridge grunted. "The carnival is miles out of town. There are convenience stores up and down the highway."

"That's what I said," the detective explained. "But she maintained it was the truth. And she said she's never seen Patti before."

"You mean she denied even talking to me behind Whit's End?" Patti asked.

The detective gazed calmly at Patti. "According to her, she didn't talk to you behind Whit's End or even at the carnival."

"What?" Patti cried out. "But I have her card. She gave me the queen of hearts!"

Detective Anderson held the card up with the very tips of his fingers and turned it around. "Unfortunately, it's a standard playing card. You could've gotten it anywhere."

"Are you saying Patti is lying?" Mr. Eldridge asked.

"I'm saying that this queen of hearts doesn't prove anything. For that matter, the jack of hearts isn't very helpful, either, unless we can match it to the rest of the deck—and its owner."

The Eldridges fumed silently. Then Mr. Eldridge asked, "What about fingerprints on the cards? Can't you check those?"

Detective Anderson shook his head. "I could check, but we probably won't find anything useful," he said. "Patti pushed the first card into her pocket several times, and she's handled both of them. Still, I could have the lab take a look if you insist."

"We wouldn't want to *inconvenience* you," Mr. Eldridge growled.

"Don't get upset," Detective Anderson said. "I believe something is going on, and I'll do everything I can to find out what it is."

There was nothing more to say, so Detective Anderson left. The phone rang just as they closed the door behind him. It was Donna Barclay.

"Aren't you coming over today?" Donna asked Patti. "I thought we were going to do our math together."

Patti looked at the kitchen clock. It was nearly 5:00 in the afternoon. "I'm sorry," she said. "I forgot. Our house was broken into last night."

Donna gasped. "Oh no! Did they steal anything?" she said.

"No," Patti answered. "That's what's so weird about it. In fact, the whole thing is really bizarre."

"Look, why don't you come over? My parents are going out to eat, so Jimmy and I are supposed to send out for pizza. You can tell me what happened. Then we can get our math out of the way."

Patti cupped her hand over the receiver and asked her mother.

Mrs. Eldridge nodded, then said, "Yes, but we'll drive you over."

"Drive me over? But I can walk," Patti said.

"We'll drive you over," Mr. Eldridge repeated firmly from the living room.

Patti suddenly understood. Her parents were worried about her but didn't want to come right out and say so.

"I'll be right over," Patti told Donna and, having said good-bye, hung up the phone.

"And you'll call us to pick you up when you're ready to come home," Mrs. Eldridge added.

****

"This is really neat," Jimmy Barclay said through a mouthful of pepperoni and extra cheese.

Donna looked at her brother with a disapproving scowl. "It *isn't neat,* Jimmy," she said. "Why don't you go eat your pizza in front of the TV or play Zappazoids in your room or something?"

"And miss this? No way!"

The three of them sat in a circle around the pizza box and yanked at the pieces inside. Donna resumed the conversation with Patti. "So they tore your house apart and you don't know why?"

Patti nodded and pulled at a long string of cheese that hung from her crust.

"I wanna go back to that part about the fortune-teller," Jimmy said. "She really put a curse on you?"

"You were at Whit's End. You heard about it," Donna reminded him.

Jimmy said impatiently, "I know, but I wanted to hear Patti say it herself. You were really cursed, Patti?"

"I'm not supposed to believe in curses," Patti said.

"But you do, don't you?" Jimmy watched her closely.

"I don't know," Patti said with a shrug. "All I know is that everything started to go wrong after I saw her."

Donna sat thoughtfully for a minute, then said, "She told the detective she did the whole curse thing as a performance. So the curse can't really work, can it?"

"A curse is a curse, even if it's put on someone as a show," Jimmy said earnestly.

"How do you know?" Donna challenged him.

"My *Dark Mysteries* comic books," he replied.

"I thought you stopped reading them when you became a Christian," she said.

"I did, but that doesn't mean I forgot everything I read in them before."

"But the curse wasn't for a show," Patti interjected. "She was lying about that. She knew who I was, and she yelled her curse at me."

"So you *do* believe in curses," Jimmy said, a wry smile stretching across his face.

"I didn't say that."

"But you do."

"Leave her alone, Jimmy," Donna said.

Jimmy went on, "But it's important, you see? She gets cursed, and then her house gets broken into. It's connected."

"No kidding, Mr. Sherlock Holmes," Donna said, jabbing him.

Jimmy grimaced. "I remember from issue 94 of *Dark Mysteries* that there was this guy who had a curse put on him by some gypsies, and later on some things were stolen from his house."

"Why?" Patti asked.

"Because the gypsy who put the curse on the other guy needed something personal to make the curse work."

Donna rolled her eyes and said, "Jimmy, what in the world are you talking about?"

"It's like voodoo," Jimmy explained. "You know, when they take a lock of your hair or a piece of your clothes and attach it to a doll that looks like you. Then they stick pins in it and you feel the pain."

"Oh, great. Thanks, Jimmy," Patti groaned.

Donna tossed a balled-up napkin at her brother. "You're not helping things," she told him.

"I'm just telling you what I read. I didn't say it was true."

"Then stick to what's true, okay? You're gonna give us nightmares," snapped Donna.

Jimmy reached for another piece of pizza. "I just think it explains why Mark's letter was stolen, that's all."

"You think Madam Clara has Mark's letter stuck to a voodoo doll of me?" Patti questioned him.

"Maybe," Jimmy said, then sipped his soda.

Patti sat silently, chewing her pizza with a worried expression.

Donna glared at her brother. "You're a real pest, do you know that?" she said. "You're scaring Patti with something we're not even supposed to believe in. Mom and Dad aren't gonna be happy that you're going around quoting old, scary comics."

Patti and Donna went up to Donna's room to do their math homework. "Don't listen to Jimmy," Donna said as they settled down on the bed with their books and notebooks. "He's got a wild imagination."

"Don't worry about it. I don't really believe in that junk," Patti said in as careless a voice as she could manage.

As the evening progressed, however, she found it harder and harder to concentrate on her work. Madam Clara and the curse kept coming to mind. And Jimmy's words kept coming back to haunt her. *That's why they stole Mark's letter,* he had said. It made sense. It was the only thing missing. Maybe there was something magical about Mark's letter that made it more powerful to the curse than anything else. Maybe it was because he was a close friend or because she missed him so much. The reasons kept going around and around in her mind. Madam Clara's curse seemed stronger than ever. What else could it do to her?

By eight o'clock, both girls were ready to call it quits with their math. Donna offered to put in a video for them to watch, but Patti wasn't in the mood. She wanted to go home. After resisting Donna's appeals to stay, Patti went to the kitchen and tried to call her parents to come pick her up. The line was busy. Twenty minutes later it was still busy, and she started to worry. Her parents were never on the phone that long. *Something is wrong at home,* she thought. *Something bad has happened.*

"What should I do?" Patti asked as she hung up the phone for the eleventh time.

"Keep trying," Donna suggested.

Ten minutes later, the line was *still* busy, and Patti decided she should walk home. She told herself, *If something is wrong, I want to be there.*

"I'll walk with you," Donna offered.

"Are you allowed to leave Jimmy home alone?"

"No."

Jimmy, who had overheard from the family room, came in and said, "Go on, Donna, I'll be all right. I'll call Oscar and ask him to come over."

Donna frowned. "You and Oscar alone in our house? You'll burn it down."

"Thanks for the vote of confidence," Jimmy said.

Patti waved the suggestion aside. "Forget it, Donna," she said.

"But your parents said you shouldn't walk home alone," Donna reminded her.

"It's okay," Patti said. "No point both of us getting in trouble. I'll run. It isn't very far."

Jimmy said, "If you cut through the woods, it's real quick. Just watch out for the creek. It's deeper than it looks."

"I know, Jimmy. I didn't just move here," Patti said impatiently.

Jimmy looked at her for a moment, then scratched at his curly, brown hair. "Boy, Donna, you and Patti'll make great friends," he said. "She's starting to talk to me in the same obnoxious tone you use."

Donna smiled. "You bring it out in people, Jimmy."

"Thanks for inviting me over," Patti said to Donna at the door.

"I'm glad you came. Sorry about all your trouble." She hesitated as if she wasn't sure of what to say next. Finally, she added, "I'd like you to come over again. If you want to. I mean, it's up to you."

"Look, Donna, you don't have to be my friend just because Mr. Whittaker asked you to."

Donna looked confused. "Mr. Whittaker didn't ask me to be your friend," she said. "What made you think that?"

"Connie said that Mr. Whittaker was worried about me, and . . ." Patti started to explain. Donna's expression left no room to doubt that she didn't know what Patti was talking about. She gave up. "I'd like to come over again," she said finally. "Maybe we can do something better than our math homework."

"We can tackle Jimmy and put masking tape over his mouth."

"It's a deal!" Patti laughed and walked across the porch to the steps. As she made her way to the street, she felt an odd sensation somewhere deep inside. Apart from Jimmy scaring her, she enjoyed being with Donna. It wasn't awkward or forced. They talked about a lot of different things—not just girl stuff—and seemed to have much in common. Maybe, just maybe, they really could be friends.

Patti crossed the street and walked down to the edge of the woods. She had made it only a few steps inside when she realized it was a bad idea. The woods were already a wall of darkness, with the trees standing like stark shadows. She imagined that if she was really under some kind of curse, walking through dark woods at night was the last thing she should do.

She glanced back at the Barclay house and wondered if she should go back in and call her parents. *The phone's probably still busy,* she thought. *If something's wrong, I need to get there right now.* Having made up her mind, she strode quickly around the edge of the woods, keeping close to the patchy yellow glow of the streetlights. She hummed softly to herself. At some point in her childhood, she had decided that nothing bad could happen to you if you hummed.

Halfway home, she came upon Wilkins Park, a small grove

of trees with a play area for children. It was almost as dark as the woods—the one or two lamps on the path had burned out—but she knew it was only a short distance. To go around it meant either venturing farther into the woods or jumping the Frazinis' fence and cutting across their backyard. Mr. Frazini was well known for yelling at kids who cut through his yard, so Patti decided to go straight through the park.

She weaved her way past the merry-go-round and the triple seesaws when suddenly, something rattled to her right. She glanced over at the swings. They moved gently in the evening breeze as if being ridden by ghosts.

"Stop it," she told herself as she picked up her pace. "I don't believe in ghosts or curses or—"

Just then she heard a loud *bang!* Patti nearly jumped out of her skin. It sounded as if something hard had hit the slide off to the right. This was followed by a *rat-a-tat-tat* as if a rock were skidding and bouncing down the length of the metal board. A branch in the tree above it rustled.

A squirrel must've dropped an acorn, she assured herself as she went from a brisk jog to a furious sprint. Her heart pounded. *Oh, please, let it be a squirrel,* she wished, as if the curse had sprung legs and was chasing her.

Subdued panic pumped energy through her body and pushed her to the other end of the park. Clearing that, she raced up a small hillside toward the road and its welcoming light.

"Ah!" she cried as her left foot caught the edge of a rock. Sprawling to the ground, she threw her arms out to try to catch herself. Her math book and notebook flew away. She landed on her left arm, her elbow jabbing squarely into her stomach. It knocked the wind out of her.

The night exploded into pinpoints of light. The pain was excruciating. Patti tried to breathe in, but she couldn't. She rolled onto her back and gasped for air. It was awful. Seconds became long, wheezing minutes. The grass was damp and cold and clung to her jacket.

Blinded by the agony and the deep covering of the incline, she could only sense that someone was coming near. She thought it was her imagination at first. But the shadow moved. Not only did it move, but it moved unmistakably toward her from the woods. *Who is it?* she wondered helplessly as her lungs screamed for air. She managed to roll over again to get to her feet. The wet grass was no friend to her tennis shoes, and she slipped, crashing down again.

This is the curse, she thought in her fear. *I can't fight it. I can't even breathe. And now Madam Clara will get whatever it is she wants from me.*

The figure was closer now, bending down, its hands reaching out for her.

Her eyes adjusted and looked into its face. Now she knew she was done for, because the face she saw made no sense. It was all wrong, totally impossible. It absolutely didn't belong here. It was a trick of the curse.

"Are you all right?" Mark Prescott asked in a bewildered tone.

CHAPTER NINE

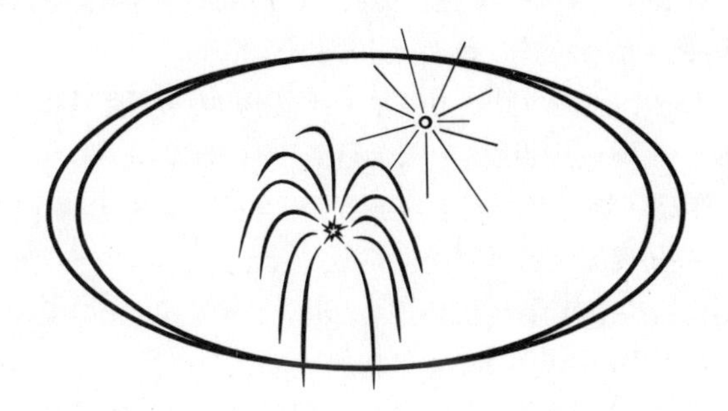

"Take it easy," Mark said quietly as he knelt next to her. "Calm down. Just try to breathe slowly."

Patti eventually worked some air back into her lungs. After another minute, she was able to sit up.

Mark leaned close to her. "What happened to you?" he asked.

"I fell down," Patti croaked.

"I figured that much."

Patti took a few more deep breaths. Her vision cleared, but now her head hurt. She turned to face Mark, and for a moment she still couldn't believe it was him. But there he was, kneeling next to her. He pushed his dark hair off his forehead—an old habit of his.

"Are you okay now?" he asked.

"Yeah," she replied. Then she punched him in the arm.

"Ow!" he cried out as he fell backward. "What's that for?"

"For scaring the living daylights out of me!"

Holding his arm, Mark stood up. "You're welcome!" he said unhappily.

She reached out her hand for him to help her stand. He grabbed it and, though she expected him to give it a hard yank in revenge for the punch, merely gave it enough of a pull so she could get to her feet.

"Were you following me?" she asked as she brushed off the back of her clothes.

"I went to your house, and your parents said you were at the Barclays', so I walked over there. When I got to the Barclays', Donna said you walked home. I cut through the woods because I thought that's the way you'd go."

"You didn't follow me through Wilkins Park?"

"No," he said, still rubbing his arm. They retrieved her math book and notebook and started up the hillside to the street. "Are you friends with Donna Barclay now?"

"Kind of."

"You didn't say so in your letters."

Patti turned to him, her eyes narrowing angrily. It was an expression she used only with him. "You mean you've been reading them? Thanks a lot for all your answers. What did I get? One letter. *One* letter! And I got it yesterday! How long have you been gone? Months!"

"I'm not a very good writer," he said sheepishly.

"You sure aren't!"

He said with a hint of annoyance, "Look, if you're going to nag me—"

"You deserve to be nagged," she cut in. "Some friend you turned out to be."

"Hey, I'm here, aren't I? I came to see you as soon as we got in town! You were the very first one. Give me a break." He rubbed his arm again and muttered, "Boy, you punch me, then you yell at me . . ."

In the glare of the streetlight, she could see him better. He had grown a couple of inches, though he still had the same slender physique. His face had changed, going from round boyishness to the start of the narrow shape of manhood. *He's beginning to look like his father,* she thought. She smiled without meaning to. At summer camp last year, she'd had a crush on a boy named David. That was the closest she'd come to experiencing those kinds of feelings. The truth was that she'd liked David because he seemed like an older version of Mark.

"What are you doing here anyway?" she asked.

"I'm on spring break, and my dad had to come to Odyssey on business, so—"

Patti laughed. "What kind of business would your dad have in Odyssey? He works for the federal government!"

"That's right," Mark said. "Do you know about that new building they're going to put out at Brook Meadow?"

"You mean . . .?"

Mark nodded. "My dad is a consultant on the project—he's helping them to work out the details so they can build it."

"How long are you going to be around?" Patti asked.

"Just this week . . . for now."

"For now?"

"Yeah. If my dad is transferred here after the building's done, then we'll have to move back and—"

"Move back? You mean you might move back to *Odyssey?"* She squealed and had to restrain herself from jumping up and down.

"Maybe," Mark replied, blushing at her enthusiasm.

"I don't believe it!" she shouted, and, much to their surprise, she stepped forward and hugged him.

He quickly stepped back from her and held up his hands. He looked around to make sure no one had seen it. "Patti, cut it out!" he said. "What's wrong with you?"

Patti, a little confused, studied him for a moment. "Nothing's wrong with me," she insisted. "I just got excited. Why? Don't you want to move back to Odyssey?"

He shrugged. "I don't know. Everything's happened so fast. It's kind of strange being here."

"Oh, that's right," she said indignantly. "I forgot. You have all your old pals back in Washington, D. C. You said so in your letter. You're Mr. Happy now, aren't you? Busy, busy with your cherry blossoms."

"Patti, what's gotten into you?" Mark asked, dumbfounded.

She tried to wave the question away. "Nothing. I've had a hard day. I'm tired."

"Why did you have a hard day?" Mark asked.

"Didn't my parents tell you what happened?"

They had reached her front porch now. The lights were on

inside the house. Through the front window, Patti could see her parents talking to Richard and Julie Prescott in the family room.

Mark shook his head. "Did something happen?"

"Boy, do I have a lot to tell you," she said and opened the front door.

****

Though it was getting late, the Eldridges and Prescotts gathered around the Eldridges' kitchen table for tea, coffee, and cookies.

"How's it feel being back?" Mrs. Eldridge asked as she passed the mugs of hot drinks around. Milk, creamer, and sugar were added, creating a momentary cacophony of chinking porcelain and rattling spoons. "Is the house still standing?"

Julie Prescott's mother—Mark's grandmother—had lived in Odyssey. When she died, she left the house to Julie. That's where Julie and Mark had stayed when the family had separated early last summer. It was like a second home to them.

"Mr. Wallace is taking good care of it," Julie Prescott said after sipping her tea. Mr. Wallace had been hired by the Prescotts to care for the house after Julie and Mark moved back to Washington, D. C. "It's a little strange being back. Things have changed. I noticed they started work on the new mall."

Mr. Eldridge chuckled. "That's Odyssey for you. Always on the march for progress." He turned his attention to Mark's father. "So, Richard, I'm curious about this new government complex. What's it going to be?"

Richard Prescott leaned back in his chair. "I'm not really supposed to talk about it," he replied. "You know how the government is. I guess you could call it a place for archive storage."

"Like Noah's archive?" Patti asked playfully.

"Joan of Archive," Mark corrected her. The families groaned.

"Archive storage?" Mr. Eldridge continued.

Mr. Prescott nodded. "Information, papers, computers—a place independent of Washington to keep it all filed."

"Richard was the one who suggested this area," Mrs. Prescott said proudly. "He remembered seeing Brook Meadow during one of his visits here and mentioned it to his bosses."

"I had some local help," Mr. Prescott said modestly.

"Basically you're building a big filing cabinet out at Brook Meadow," Mr. Eldridge observed wryly.

"Something like that," Mark's father said with a laugh.

"Have you chosen your computer technicians yet? You want to make sure everything is hooked up properly," Mr. Eldridge said.

"Not yet. The bids are still coming in," Mr. Prescott replied, then added as a tease, "Why? Do you know a company that's interested?"

Richard Prescott knew full well that Bob Eldridge worked for Parker Technologies, a local computer company. Mr. Eldridge smiled and said, "I'll tell my people to get in touch with your people."

Mrs. Eldridge pondered the plate of cookies, decided on one, then asked, "How do you like being back, Mark?"

Mark shrugged. "It's okay, I guess."

"Is there really a chance you might move back?" Patti's father asked Richard and Julie.

Julie looked to her husband. "Well, Richard?"

"It depends on a lot of different things," he said. "If the building project is successful, they'll want people from Washington to come manage it. I might be one of those people."

"That would be nice," Mrs. Eldridge said.

"Mark doesn't want to move back," Patti suddenly announced.

Everyone looked at her with surprise.

"What?" Julie Prescott asked, then glanced at her son. "He told you that?"

"No," Mark said firmly.

Mrs. Eldridge looked at her daughter with a knowing light in her eyes. "What makes you think he doesn't want to move back?" she asked.

"Because of his letter. All he talked about was how *happy* he is back in Washington."

Richard and Julie nearly choked on their drinks. "Happy?" Mark's father said.

"Now, wait a minute—" Mark started to say.

"He's been *miserable,*" Mrs. Prescott exclaimed.

"Mom—" Mark pleaded and held up his hand as if to say something more, but his mother didn't give him the chance.

Julie continued, "He complains that his old friends aren't like his friends anymore and says how he doesn't like school and the neighborhood has changed—"

Mr. Prescott chimed in, "'It's not like Odyssey.' Isn't that his pet phrase? Nothing's as good as Odyssey. There's no Whit's End, it's too crowded, there's too much traffic, he has nowhere to play. He never lets up. I had to suggest building the government complex here just to get some peace and quiet at home."

By now, Mark's face had turned a deep crimson. His arms were folded, and his chin was sunk into his chest.

Patti stared at him open-mouthed. "You're kidding," she managed to say.

"Thanks for the support, Mom and Dad," Mark groaned.

"So you *do* want to move back," Patti challenged him.

Mark's lips were clamped shut for a moment. Then he muttered, "Well . . . I wouldn't say *no.*"

Everyone laughed. He sank lower in his chair.

"I'd like to see that letter," said Julie Prescott.

"You can't," Patti stated.

Mr. Eldridge explained, "It's the only thing that was missing after the house was ransacked."

"That's odd," Richard Prescott mused, his brow furrowed. He absentmindedly pushed his hair away from his forehead.

Just like Mark, Patti noted. "The police don't have any clues or ideas?"

"Nothing helpful right now," Patti's father said. "We're certain it has something to do with the people at the spring carnival—Madam Clara in particular."

Mark's father thought for a moment, glanced at his watch, then sat up and said, "Look at the time. It's late. We'd better get to bed if we don't want to miss church in the morning."

They said their good nights to each other. Patti and Mark promised to talk after church about what they would do together next. Then the Prescotts were gone and the Eldridges made for bed.

In her room, Patti felt the happiest she'd been in a long time. She was extremely tired but couldn't stop smiling. Mark was back. He might even come back for good. Suddenly Madam Clara and the curse and Jimmy's comments about voodoo and her fright in the park all seemed distant and powerless. Binger, who had finally been retrieved from the trunk of the car, sat contentedly on her bed. "Isn't it great?" she asked him.

She yawned as she pulled open her dresser drawer. Her nightgown wasn't there. She then remembered that her mother had washed it. Pulling on a robe, she padded down the stairs to the laundry room to get it. Somewhere outside, fireworks exploded in the distance. *It's the last night of the spring carnival,* she thought. *They always do a fireworks display.*

She found her nightgown hanging on a rack next to the washer and dryer. As she pulled it off the hanger, she caught her reflection in the window pane directly in front of her. She ran her fingers through her hair and wondered whether she should get it cut differently. Maybe Donna Barclay would have a suggestion. Donna always looked nice.

Patti's reflection blurred abruptly. She blinked, thinking her eyes were playing tricks on her. Suddenly her face was transformed into the face of Madam Clara. The old fortune-teller leered at her through the window.

Patti screamed.

CHAPTER TEN

For the third time in 24 hours, Detective Anderson came to the Eldridges' house. "I heard the police call on my radio, and once I heard the address, I knew it was more trouble," he said.

"We're sorry to get you out so late," Mrs. Eldridge replied.

The detective shrugged it off. "A bachelor cop like me keeps all kinds of crazy hours."

"There's no one back there," Officer Stenson informed them as he entered through the back.

"Are you surprised?" Mr. Eldridge asked sarcastically. The three Eldridges were huddled on the couch. Mr. and Mrs. Eldridge wrapped their arms around Patti, whose tears were only beginning to subside, but her body continued to shake.

Patti was vaguely aware of Officer Stenson—who came as soon as Patti's father had called 911— as he signaled Detective

Anderson aside. They whispered intensely for a minute. She thought the officer handed something to the detective. Stenson then nodded and slipped out the front door.

"Well?" Mr. Eldridge asked.

Detective Anderson stood next to the couch. His overcoat hung loose and disheveled. *Was he asleep when he heard the call?* Patti wondered for no particular reason.

"Officer Stenson didn't see anyone. But he found this on the windowsill outside." The detective held up a playing card by the edges with the very tips of his fingers. It was a 10 of hearts.

"There!" Mr. Eldridge snapped. "What kind of proof do you need now?"

Detective Anderson turned the card around. The design on the back was completely unlike that on the other two cards. "I still need more than this," he said.

Patti's father grunted. "I don't care if they're identical or different or printed on dollar bills! I just want this harassment to stop! If you won't go out to the carnival and take care of it, I will!"

"You're upset, and I don't blame you," the detective said patiently. "But you can't take the law into your own hands. Neither can I. I'll go to the carnival and check things out. I'll talk to Madam Clara again. I'll even have this card checked for fingerprints. But I'm not hopeful of finding anything that'll help."

"It has to stop," Mr. Eldridge said more softly.

"Tonight's the last night of the carnival. These characters

have to pack up and move on to their next site. Maybe this trouble will move on with them."

"Is that it?" Mr. Eldridge said, mostly as an appeal. "Madam Clara and her pals can harass us and then just skip town? Is that justice?"

"Justice is administered based on solid evidence, Mr. Eldridge, *which* we don't have right now," Detective Anderson said firmly. "Apart from this card, we can't even find evidence that Madam Clara was out there. One could argue that Patti is tired and imagined seeing that face in the window."

"And the card?" Mrs. Eldridge demanded.

"I'm not saying one way or another," the detective said. "Girls Patti's age are often at the mercy of wild emotions. I've seen it again and again. They do things to get attention."

Mr. Eldridge leaped to his feet. "All of this is Patti's attempt to get attention?" he almost shouted. "Is that what you're saying? She tore up the house to get attention?"

"No, Mr. Eldridge, that was real enough. But—"

"But what? Are you a detective or a psychiatrist?" Mr. Eldridge snapped. "I resent you coming in here and making comments like that. My daughter is perfectly stable and certainly not the kind of person who would resort to *this* to get attention."

"It's voodoo," Patti whispered.

"What?" her mother asked.

"This is all because of the curse. They're playing tricks on me to scare me. It's voodoo," Patti said, then began to cry again.

Detective Anderson gestured toward Patti as if to silently say to her parents, "See? Your daughter has problems."

Mr. Eldridge looked helplessly at his daughter, then showed the detective to the door. He apologized for getting angry. "I know you're doing everything you can," he concluded.

"We'll make sure a patrol car stays in the area for the next few days," Detective Anderson assured him.

Even with a mild sleeping tablet, Patti couldn't sleep. The old woman's face in the window came back to her time and again. "You didn't listen to me," she imagined Madam Clara saying. "You didn't believe in the curse."

****

The next morning, Patti went to her parents' Sunday school class rather than her own. She knew the kids were all talking about what had happened, and she couldn't face them. It was better that way for Mark, too. The kids could give him all their attention. Patti barely heard the teacher's lesson. She felt drained and detached. "Be anxious for nothing," someone read from the Bible. "Perfect love casts out all fear," someone else read. Patti picked up on those words because she knew the verses. "God, help me," she prayed.

The Prescotts sat with the Eldridges in the church service. Pastor Henderson made a special mention of the difficulties the Eldridges had been experiencing and led the congregation in a moment of prayer for them. At one point, Mark reached over and held her hand. It took all her energy to keep from collapsing into heaving sobs.

I'm being overdramatic, she kept telling herself. *I'm making a big deal out of nothing. Maybe I was tired and only* thought *I saw Madam Clara in the window. It might have been my imagination.*

Where Patti would normally stay to socialize after the church service, today she wanted to make a quick escape. Her parents sensed it and ushered her out a side door to their car. The Prescotts followed close behind. Mr. Whittaker was the only one who made a point of chasing them down, and that was to say that he was sorry about the break-in and was praying for them all.

"I hope you'll come see me at my shop," Mr. Whittaker said to the Prescotts while pulling Mark close for a hug.

"We will," Richard Prescott promised.

Mr. Eldridge surprised Patti by opening the trunk and pulling out Binger. He dropped the bear onto the seat next to her and said, "I had a feeling you might need him today."

She hugged Binger, then her father, and promised, "I'll be okay. I'm feeling better now. I'm sorry to be such a wreck."

Her father stroked her hair. "You've had a couple of bad days," he said. "You're allowed to be a wreck."

Mark climbed into the car. "Are you okay?" he asked.

Patti shrugged. "I guess so."

"You're not too tired?" It was a leading question. Mark was up to something.

"Too tired? For what?"

"Me and my mom and dad decided to kidnap your family. We figured we should get you away for a while. We're going up to Trickle Lake for a picnic," he announced.

The two families conferred for a couple of minutes. Mr. Eldridge and Mr. Prescott spoke earnestly about something; then they got into their cars and drove off.

"But I'm not dressed for a picnic," Patti told her parents.

"I put a change of clothes in the trunk," Mrs. Eldridge informed her.

"You knew we were going to do this?"

"We talked to the Prescotts about it on the phone this morning while you were in the shower. They're very worried about us."

To get to Trickle Lake, they had to pass Brook Meadow. The carnival was in various stages of being disassembled. The Ferris wheel looked like an upright pie out of which someone had taken a big piece. The merry-go-round, the games, and the stalls were all being taken down by the workers. *Good,* Patti thought. *Good-bye and good riddance.* For the first time, she was glad the government had bought the land. She never wanted to see a carnival there again.

Mr. Eldridge switched on the turn signal and slowed down.

"What are you doing?" Patti asked, suddenly worried.

"Richard and I want to look around the carnival. He needs to look at the grounds for the building, and I want to see if I can find anything the police missed."

"No, Dad, I don't want to go there," Patti protested. "Please don't."

Mr. Eldridge looked at her in the rearview mirror. "You don't have to," he said. "I'm going to drop you off at the diner just down the road. You don't think I'd really make you see that place again, do you?"

Patti sighed with relief and pulled Binger close.

At the diner, the two dads said good-bye to their families and drove off for the carnival in Richard Prescott's rental car. Mrs. Eldridge pulled a bag of clothes for Patti out of the trunk of the car. "You can change in the women's rest room," she suggested.

Patti stood at the back of the car with Binger in her arms.

"Nice bear," Mark said.

Patti couldn't tell if he was being sincere or sarcastic. "I like him, so watch what you say," she warned playfully.

"Do you want to take him into the diner?" Mrs. Eldridge asked, her hand on the trunk lid.

Patti thought about it, then said, "No."

"Then let's put him inside."

"Poor Binger," Patti said sadly as she gently laid him in the trunk. "He always gets stuck in here."

Mrs. Eldridge closed the lid.

The diner was crowded with a Sunday lunch bunch that looked like an equal mixture of families on their way home from church and truck drivers who'd stopped in for some good, old-fashioned cooking. Mark and Patti and their mothers sat down at a Formica-topped table with chrome siding. The red cushions on the metal-framed chairs were split and cracked, but comfortable. A blonde woman with too much makeup and a red-striped outfit took their orders for two sodas and two coffees. Mark flipped over his placemat and began to play a children's name-the-states game on the back. Patti flipped hers over and borrowed a pen from her mother so she could play connect-the-dots. The picture turned out to be a sailboat.

"Is it too early in the year to rent a paddleboat at Trickle Lake?" Julie Prescott wondered aloud.

Mrs. Eldridge smiled. "That's a good idea," she said. "We'll see."

Patti was showing Mark her sailboat when her eye was caught by a glimmer outside. A large truck passed by. It was loaded with a ride from the carnival. She followed it until it was gone, then noticed that a stranger was standing next to their car. He turned slightly, enough for Patti to see that it was the man from the shooting gallery. Patti gasped.

Mark leaned forward on the table and asked, "What's wrong?"

"That man," Patti said softly. "He runs the shooting gallery."

"Really?" Mark strained to see. "Are you sure?"

Patti nodded. "How could I forget?"

Susan Eldridge and Julie Prescott were both looking now. "What's he doing out there?" Patti's mother asked.

"Nothing," Mark replied. "He's just standing there."

"Looks suspicious to me," Mrs. Prescott said.

Just then a black-and-white police car pulled into the parking lot. Oblivious to those watching him from the diner—or the man next to the Eldridges' car—an officer climbed out. He squinted at the sunlight, put on a dark pair of sunglasses, adjusted the belt on his uniform, and strode toward the entrance. The shooting-gallery man saw him and walked away.

"That was interesting," Mrs. Prescott said as relief washed over the four of them.

"Do you think he was going to do something to the car?" Patti asked.

Mark frowned. "Why would he? I mean, how could he know it was your car?"

"That's true. How could he?" Mrs. Eldridge said. "It must've been a coincidence. The carnival isn't far from here."

Patti suddenly remembered that she hadn't told anyone about the girl at the carnival who looked like her or the way the shooting-gallery man had watched the Eldridges drive away. "He knows our car. He saw us leave the carnival," she said.

"I wish your father would hurry," Julie Prescott said to Mark.

Mark tapped the table excitedly. "I sure wish I knew what was going on. This whole thing is so weird."

"No kidding," Patti said.

Mrs. Eldridge held up the bag with Patti's clothes in it. "Why don't you go into the rest room and change so we'll be ready to leave when the men get back?" she suggested.

Patti agreed, took the bag, and followed a sign with an arrow that said "Rest Rooms." It led her down a small hallway at the back of the diner. She pushed open the

"Ladies" door and went past the three stalls to a large sink on the other wall. Glancing at her reflection in the mirror mounted above, she noticed that she had the start of dark circles under her eyes. *Not enough sleep,* she thought. *Tonight I have to get some sleep.*

No one else was in the rest room, so she decided to change quickly right where she was. She kicked off her nice shoes and pulled her jeans on under her church dress. She then unbuttoned the top of the dress, pulled it over her head, and shoved it into the bag. Yanking on the sweatshirt her mother had brought, Patti smiled. *Mom thinks of everything,* she thought. *Trickle Lake is always cool since it's up on the mountain.*

Her head popped up through the top of the sweatshirt, and she noticed a woman had come into the rest room. The woman turned and smiled at Patti.

Patti thought her heart had stopped. "Madam Clara!" she cried.

"Hello, child."

"Don't come near me or I'll scream so loud that the policeman will come in," Patti threatened.

"You don't have to scream *again,*" the fortune-teller said gently. "You nearly gave this poor old woman a heart attack when you screamed last night."

"Gave *you* a heart attack! What do you think you did to me?" Patti complained. Somehow this slight old woman didn't seem like anyone to be afraid of. Patti felt anger more than fear.

The woman spread her arms in appeal. "What can I do? How else can I reach you?"

"Don't you have phones?" Patti asked, strengthened by her anger. "Can't you use the front door like normal people?"

"Phones and front doors involve your parents. This is between us, child. It is private. Your visit to me set into motion unfortunate events. For that, I'm sorry. Yet, I've been trying to help you, and you keep making it very difficult."

"Help me! You put a curse on me!"

"I cursed your lack of faith in me, your betrayal of me when I needed you." The woman grinned crookedly. "It has not been pleasant for either of us, let me assure you. But I'm here now to help you eliminate the curse."

"How?" Patti asked warily.

"By reversing the spell. But you must assist me."

"Assist you how?"

The woman took a step forward, then stopped as if she suddenly remembered Patti would scream. "I need an item. Something personal, which I can use to reverse the spell," she explained.

"I get it. This is like voodoo, right?"

"If you insist."

"You already got that letter from my room. What else do you want?"

"Child, I do not have your letter. How could I possibly get a letter from your room?"

"When you vandalized our house!"

"I did no such thing. It is obviously the result of the curse.

But we can stop it. An item, child."

"Like what?"

Madam Clara tapped her shriveled cheek thoughtfully. "Something that is important to you. What do you treasure the most?"

Patti had to think about it. "I have some pictures . . . books . . . presents people have given me . . . a china ballerina that your curse broke when it trashed my house . . ."

"It must be something larger. Think, child. It must be valuable to your heart."

Finally Patti thought of it. "Binger. My stuffed bear. The bear you made me win."

The fortune-teller cackled. "The bear will be perfect. Bring it to me."

"And you'll make the curse go away?"

"I will."

Patti was suddenly defiant. "What if I don't believe in your stupid curse? What if I said I thought you keep making these bad things happen?"

Again, Patti thought Madam Clara might step closer, but she hesitated. Instead, she pushed her face forward and hissed, "Suit yourself, child. If you do not bring me that bear, I can promise that the curse will extend to you, your family, and your friends. This curse is like a cancer that will spread to all whom you love. A vandalized house and a few broken trinkets are nothing compared to what will befall you!"

"I'm not afraid of you," Patti said, but she was suddenly aware that her knees were shaking.

"Be wise, child. You must do what I say, and then you'll be done with it. Bring me the bear or you'll hurt as you've never known it before! And you must say nothing about this—to anyone—or the curse will not be halted! Do you understand?"

In spite of herself, Patti nodded her head. The woman spoke with such passion that Patti didn't dare refuse her. Images of her parents' death—an accident or a fire—worked through her mind.

"Now, you must bring it to me tonight at the carnival," Madam Clara said.

"Tonight!" Patti said. "Why can't I give it to you now?"

Madam Clara backed toward the door. "Tonight. And then you can live the rest of your life in peace. And . . . not a word!"

The rest room door opened and nearly hit Madam Clara in the back. A startled customer said, "I'm sorry."

Madam Clara glared as she brushed past the woman and disappeared down the hallway. Patti noticed that she didn't go in the direction of the dining room but the opposite way, toward the rear emergency exit. The customer slipped into one of the stalls.

Patti thought she might throw up. *What am I going to do?* she asked herself. She waited a moment to try to get her strength back. She knew she couldn't return to the table looking scared.

The door opened again, and Patti's mother peeked in. "What are you doing, dressing for Cinderella's ball?" she asked. “Your father and Richard are back. We’re ready to leave.”

“I’ll be right out,” Patti said.

Mrs. Eldridge paused. “Are you all right?”

Patti nodded quickly. “Uh huh. I . . . I just felt tired all of a sudden.”

“You can sleep on a blanket up at Trickle Lake. The sun will feel wonderful now,” her mother said.

Patti managed a slight smile, and her mother left.

What am I going to do? she wondered.

CHAPTER ELEVEN

Trickle Lake was even cooler than they had expected, though the sun shone brightly in a blue sky. The paddleboats were still locked up in the concession shed for the winter—they wouldn't be brought out until May, when the rangers would reopen the station for the tourist season, a sign said. The two families had to entertain themselves with Frisbee® throwing, a wild football game without rules, and the food Julie Prescott had brought. It was fun for them all, in spite of their troubles. The only one who seemed unable to shake a dark mood was Richard Prescott. He had seemed preoccupied ever since they left the diner.

Patti fell back onto one of the blankets and, in the golden warmth of sunlight and the smells of spring, dozed fitfully. She dreamed of her times at Trickle Lake with Mark last summer. Here they had found a secret cave that Mark ultimately gave to a group called the Israelites to use as a hideout. Patti nearly hadn't forgiven Mark for that betrayal.

That summer was filled with all kinds of adventures for the two of them. Not all were rough-and-tumble, though. Many affected Patti's heart profoundly and made her realize she was changing. She was growing up. In just three months, she had gone from being a tough tomboy who had given that bully Joe Devlin a good stomping (on the day she met Mark) to being a blubbering girl (the day Mark moved away). She'd never cried so hard as on the day Mark left. It hurt her more than she could've anticipated.

"You'll know hurt as you've never known it before," Madam Clara had said. The words returned in her dreams. Once again, she had been put in the position of keeping a secret from her parents while trying to decide whether to give Madam Clara what she wanted. If she did—if she could sneak the bear out to the carnival site—the nightmare might end. If she didn't—if she refused to believe in Madam Clara and her powers—terrible things could happen.

"Patti?" a voice whispered. "Patti, wake up."

Patti opened her eyes.

Her mother was leaning over her. "You were having a bad dream. You were moaning," Susan Eldridge said.

"Was I?" Patti asked, then yawned. "I don't remember." Slowly she sat up. Her father and Mr. and Mrs. Prescott were stretched out on various blankets, fast asleep. Mark was sitting nearby, looking incredibly bored. When he saw that Patti was awake, his face lit up and he strolled over to her.

"Do you want to take a walk?" Mark asked.

Patti said "Sure" and stood up. Her head was still fuzzy

from her nap. "Where do you want to go?"

"Let's go see the secret cave," he said.

They walked toward the woods. "Be careful in there! You remember what happened last time!" Mrs. Eldridge called out. Last summer, Patti had fallen down a mine shaft and broken her arm.

"So what's wrong?" Mark asked her directly once they were out of earshot of the adults.

"What do you mean?"

"Something's been bothering you ever since we left the diner," Mark said.

She thought about it, then decided she couldn't even tell Mark right now. "I'm just tired," she stated simply.

Farther up the path away from the lake, they passed a large tree with graffiti carved into it. Neither of them looked at the tree directly, though Patti was sure she saw Mark glance at it out of the corner of his eye. Patti had carved a heart in the tree with the words *Patti & Mark 4 Ever.* She did it when she first realized she had a crush on him but had no idea how to act about it. It seemed so childish to her now.

Mark didn't even mention the tree, and neither did Patti. But she knew they were both thinking about it.

They reached the secret cave—"secret" because it was naturally hidden from sight by thick underbrush—and had to work extra hard to push through the thick, green curtain to the darkness inside.

It was too dark to see very well. Mark bumped into a wooden crate. A candle fell to the ground. "Maybe there are matches," he said and felt around for a pack. He found a small box near the cave wall. They felt damp and, as expected, had been there too long to be of any use.

"Well, here it is," Patti said, looking into the darkness.

"What happened to the Israelites?" Mark asked. The Israelites was the name of a group of kids Whit had established to do "good deeds" around the town.

Patti found the remnants of a glass lantern top. "Whit broke them up when school started."

Mark shook his head. "It seems like a long time ago."

Sitting down on the upended crate, Patti said, "It *was* a long time ago. It feels like everything's changed since you left."

Mark turned to face Patti, though they could barely see each other in the darkness. "I'm sorry I didn't write to you more," he said. "It was so hard being back in my old neighborhood that I figured all I'd do is gripe and complain. To tell the truth, I didn't want you to know that I didn't like being back there. I was glad Mom and Dad were together again, but I wanted them to be together *here*."

"In this cave?" Patti joked.

"Cut it out. You know what I mean."

"Yeah, I know," she said softly.

She suddenly remembered a time when she'd abruptly asked Mark to kiss her. She wished that he would try to now. But he wouldn't. She knew that she was just a friend to him, no matter what he was to her. She wondered what would happen if she blurted out that she thought she loved him. He'd probably say she was off her rocker and run out of the cave. So she kept her mouth shut. This was one secret she *had* to keep to herself.

Without any light, it was pointless to stay in the cave. They walked back toward the picnic. Near the edge of the woods, Patti sniffed the air and said, "I smell smoke."

Mark said he could smell it, too. "Someone must be burning leaves."

"Up here?" Patti asked. "And in the spring?"

Through a break in the trees, they could see smoke rising into the sky. It came from very near to where their families had been picnicking.

"Come on," Mark said quickly and took off. Patti matched his speed, and they reached the picnic area at the same time. A few yards off to the right was a meadow thick with dried grass and weeds. It was on fire. Patti's and Mark's fathers were frantically hitting at the flames with their jackets. Julie Prescott raced toward the meadow with a bucket of water she'd apparently retrieved from the empty ranger station. Susan Eldridge came from the lake with another bucketful.

"Find a container—anything! Get some water to put out this fire!" Mrs. Eldridge said. "I called the fire department."

"Drench your jacket and use it to hit the flames," Mark shouted to Patti, and then he ran off to the ranger station to find a bucket.

But that'll ruin it, Patti thought as she rushed over to her blanket and grabbed her jacket. As she picked it up, a king of hearts fell out of the pocket.

****

With flashing lights and blaring sirens, members and equipment from both the Odyssey Fire Department and the Forestry Department fire station arrived within 10 minutes. Five minutes after that, they had the fire under control. It was completely put out no more than a half hour later.

"What happened?" a uniformed fireman named Steve asked as the crews began stowing their gear.

"We don't know," Mr. Eldridge replied. "We were resting over on our blankets when suddenly we smelled smoke. Then we saw the flames in the field. That's when we called you from the ranger station and tried to put it out ourselves."

"Thank you," fireman Steve said. "I'm sorry about your clothes. I'm afraid you'll have a hard time getting them clean again."

"Don't worry about that," Mr. Prescott said.

"Any idea what might have caused it?" Mr. Eldridge asked.

Fireman Steve shook his head. "I was hoping you could tell me. You weren't barbecuing, were you? Maybe decided to roast marshmallows on a fire?"

"No, sir," Mr. Eldridge answered.

Fireman Steve scratched his balding head. "It's the wrong time of year for a brush fire, so it beats the tar out of me what—"

"Steve!" another fireman called out. He emerged from the woods, holding up a large, red gas can. With it was a large rag. "Look what I found!"

"Somebody *set* the fire?" Mrs. Prescott gasped.

"No doubt about it," the second fireman said as he approached. "This one was done on purpose."

Fireman Steve addressed the two families. "Any idea who might've done it? Were you all here when it started?"

"The kids were up in the woods," Mrs. Eldridge said before she realized how it sounded.

"Were you?" fireman Steve said suspiciously to Mark and Patti. "Doing what?"

"We were exploring in a cave," Patti explained.

"The fire was already going when we walked back," Mark added.

"Uh huh. Gotcha. Well, I'm going to have to get your names and numbers anyway for my report. A clear case of arson can't be ignored. And thanks again for being so conscientious." Fireman Steve tipped an imaginary hat and walked away.

Mrs. Eldridge groaned. "Is it never going to end?" she said.

"Do you think your 'friends' from the carnival had something to do with this?" Julie Prescott asked incredulously.

"You can bet on it," Patti's father said angrily.

"But why?" Mrs. Eldridge asked. "What do they want from us?"

Patti knew. They wanted Binger. And they wouldn't stop harassing them until they had him. In that instant, Patti determined what she had to do: anything to stop the curse.

CHAPTER TWELVE

They left Trickle Lake feeling as if they'd suffered a bad end to what was otherwise a very nice day.

Mr. Eldridge suggested that Patti ride with the Prescotts, then said, "I'll take all our things home, and then we want to go to the police station and talk to Detective Anderson. He has to see that we're in a potentially life-threatening situation. I want police protection for my family."

Patti had never seen her father so angry. It made her anxious enough to consider telling him about the king of hearts in her jacket and the encounter with Madam Clara at the diner. But she didn't. Madam Clara had been very clear with her threat. Patti couldn't tell a soul or there'd be worse trouble. All she had to do was work out the plan.

"I think I want to go home," Patti said. She figured she could move more freely if she was alone. She could sneak off to the carnival while her parents went to the police station.

"No," her father said. "I want you to be *with* someone at

all times. I don't know what Madam Clara and her thugs are up to, but I won't leave you alone to find out."

"Can I take Binger with me?" Patti asked.

"Sure you can," Mr. Eldridge replied. The two families parted after Patti got Binger back out of the trunk.

After a stop at the store to pick up some food for an evening meal, the Prescotts returned with Patti to their house—the one Mark's grandmother left to them. As soon as he had a chance, Mark nearly dragged Patti up to his old room.

"Okay, what's going on?" he demanded in a harsh whisper.

Patti feigned innocence. "What do you mean?"

"Cut it out, Patti. You know what I mean. You've been quiet ever since the diner, and I can see in your eyes that the wheels in your little brain are turning. You're thinking. You're up to something."

"I am not! Why can't everyone leave me alone?"

Julie Prescott appeared in the door. "Are you two fighting again?" she asked.

"Kind of," Mark said.

"Just like old times," Patti said, smiling weakly.

"I want to try to wash our jackets. Maybe we can get all the dirt and soot out," Mrs. Prescott said. "Clean out your pockets and bring them down to me." Then she disappeared again.

"Tell me, Patti!" Mark insisted when she was gone. He picked up his jacket and began going through the pockets.

"I don't know what you're talking about," Patti said,

following suit. She lifted her jacket and dug into the pockets. There were tissues and small slips of paper. She pulled them out. The king of hearts fell on the floor.

Mark instinctively bent to pick it up for her. Patti scrambled to get there first. "I've got it," she said.

Her fingers were nearly on the card when Mark stamped his foot down on it.

"Get off!" she cried out and tried to push him away.

He pushed her back, and in the single second it took for her to regain her balance, he snatched the card from the floor. "A king of hearts?" he said quizzically, turning the card over.

"It's mine. Give it back."

"Wait a minute," he said, a light dawning in his mind. "Weren't the cards from that fortune-teller something-of-hearts? Queen of hearts . . . the jack of hearts on your windowsill . . ."

"Just hand it over."

"Where did you get this, Patti?"

"None of your business." Her hand was still outstretched for the card.

"*When* did you get this?"

"I can't tell you," Patti said angrily. "Now give it back."

Mark wouldn't give up. "The diner. Did Madam What's-Her-Name give it to you?"

"No, she didn't," Patti answered truthfully.

Mark tossed the card to her and slumped down onto his bed. "Come on, Patti. I could ask a hundred questions and sooner or later get the truth out of you. I won't give up. You know that. Why don't you save us all the trouble and just tell me now?"

Patti thought carefully. She wanted to tell him, but she was afraid. Then it occurred to her that the only way she could get to the carnival site was with Mark's help. She decided to tell him. "I'll tell you if you promise you won't tell anyone else."

"I won't promise anything until I know what's going on."

Patti had to accept that. "I found the card in my jacket at the fire. I don't know how it got there—or when. But it was a warning to me or a threat. Both, I guess."

"From who? Madam What's-Her-Name?"

"Clara, yeah. She came into the rest room at the diner when I was changing."

"Patti!" Mark nearly shouted. "Why didn't you tell us?"

"Because she told me the curse would get even bigger if I did."

"Curse! Are you nuts? You don't believe in curses. Did you stop going to Sunday school after I left? Did you give up church? You know better than to believe in curses!"

"I don't know what I believe now, Mark. Call it a curse, call it whatever you want, but it won't stop until she gets what she wants from me. I know that. The break-in, the looking in my window, the fire . . ."

"What does she want?"

"She said she'll reverse the curse if—"

Mark interrupted her. "I don't believe this. *Reverse* the *curse?"*

"Just listen to me, will you? She said she'll reverse the curse if I give her something very personal, something I treasure more than anything else."

Mark paused to eye her curiously. "Yeah? What?"

Mrs. Prescott shouted from downstairs, "I want your jackets now!"

"Coming!" Mark called back. Somewhere in the house, a phone rang. "We're not done with this," he said as he grabbed their jackets to run them downstairs.

Her mind twisted and turned like a roller coaster through her options. She could take Binger and go to the bus stop on the corner. There was a bus to Connellsville every half hour until 9:00 at night. It went right past Brook Meadow. She could have the driver stop so she could get out and take the bear to Madam Clara. She could walk to the diner and call her parents to come get her. She'd be in big trouble, but she figured she'd be in trouble anyway. At least this way they'd be safe again.

"Patti!" Mark called loudly.

Patti went to the top of the stairs. "Yeah?"

"Come down here, please."

Please? she thought. *Mark said please?* It worried her. She went downstairs and into the kitchen. Mrs. Prescott was putting on her coat. Mr. Prescott and Mark watched Patti with worried expressions.

"What's wrong?" she asked, her eyes moving from one person to another. Richard Prescott sat on the chair in front of Patti so he could see her face better. She thought for a second what a handsome man he was. A grown-up Mark. "What?" she asked him.

"Your parents just called. They've been in a car accident."

Patti felt her knees buckle. Mr. Prescott grabbed her and guided her to a chair. "It's nothing serious," he said. "They're all right. They were on their way here from the police station when the brakes suddenly gave out. They went off the road and into a ditch. They've got some bumps and bruises, that's all. Do you hear me? They're all right."

Patti sat there, stunned and unable to make sense of the news.

Mark's father continued. "The car can't be driven, so Julie is going to get them and take them to the hospital, just to check them over. She'll bring them back here. You're going to stay here with me and Mark while she goes."

"What? I don't understand. Why?"

"Because I think this accident is related to everything else that's happened to you. You're safer here with me and Mark than out on the road." He stood up. "Your parents are okay, Patti. Don't worry. Come on, Julie, I want to check *our* car before you go anywhere in it."

Julie Prescott kissed Patti on the top of her head. "It'll be all right," she said. She and Mr. Prescott went out to the garage.

Patti felt dizzy and nauseated. "I think I'm going to be sick," she said and rushed into the downstairs bathroom. She leaned over the toilet, but nothing happened. After a moment, she turned to the sink and splashed some water on her face.

She went back out to the kitchen, where Mark still waited for her alone.

"I have to do something *right now,*" she said urgently.

"Calm down," Mark said. "There's nothing you can do."

"But there is!" she cried. "I can take Madam Clara what she wants! It's the only way to stop this curse!"

Mark shook his head. "You're delirious."

"It won't go away until I give it to her. Don't you understand?"

"What does she want?" Mark asked again.

"Something personal," Patti replied.

"I got that part. But what exactly are you going to give her—a hairbrush? Dirty socks?"

"My teddy bear," Patti said.

"All this trouble will stop if you give them their teddy bear back? But that doesn't make any sense!"

"I don't care. Are you going to help me or not?" It wasn't a question; it was an ultimatum.

Mark stood up to his full height. "I sure am! As soon as my dad comes in, I'm going to tell him everything. He'll know what to do." As if on cue, the Prescotts' rental car started up and Mrs. Prescott drove it away.

"No! You can't!" Patti begged. "He'll tell the police, he'll make a big deal out of it, and then things'll get worse."

"They can't get worse if our parents and the police know," Mark said earnestly.

"Wanna bet? This curse is real. Madam Clara is serious."

"And you're off your rocker," Mark said. "I'm sorry,

Patti, but it isn't a curse. It sounds like some kind of blackmail."

"But *why?"*

"I don't know. But we can't handle this alone. I'm going to tell my dad. Are you coming with me?"

She folded her arms and said sternly, "No."

"Okay, then I'm going to do it." He headed for the garage. Patti immediately raced up the stairs to Mark's room to get Binger. She thought she might make it back down the stairs and out the front door by the time Mark and Mr. Prescott returned. She glanced at her watch. It was 8:30. It wasn't too late to catch the Connellsville bus. She grabbed the bear just as a door slammed somewhere downstairs. *Too late,* she thought and considered sneaking out the window.

"Patti!" Mark shouted in a shrill, panicked voice. "Run! Patti—" His voice was suddenly cut off as if someone had snuffed it like a candle.

Patti rushed back out into the hall but didn't call back. Something had happened. She waited. The house was silent. The front door banged open, and Patti positioned herself to where she could see it from the top of the stairs. She put her hand over her mouth to keep from screaming. The man from the shooting gallery had grabbed Mark.

Mark bit the man's hand so he had to uncover Mark's mouth. "Run!" Mark screamed.

Another man Patti had never seen before came in through the front door, glanced around, then started up the stairs. Patti retreated to Mark's room, slammed and locked the door, and tried to think. What should she do? Heavy footsteps pounded up the stairs, then stopped at the top as if the man had paused to listen. Still clutching Binger, she looked out the window. It led out onto a small section of roof that angled with the gutter into the main section of the house. There was no one below. She opened the window.

The man in the hall jiggled the door handle furiously. Then he banged on the door. Patti was halfway out the window when he began to throw his full weight against the door. It was an old house, and the door was made of solid wood. It would hold him off at least a minute or two.

Patti carefully crept along the slender section of roof. When she reached the gutter spout, she looked below. All was quiet, even though the man continued to bash at the door. She dropped Binger into a bush, then grabbed the spout for her climb down the back of the house. Her feet soon touched ground, and she grabbed Binger. A loud *crack* told her that the man had gotten into the room. There was no time for her to wait.

She pulled Binger from the bush, then turned to escape. But as she did, strong hands grabbed her from behind and dragged her into the shadows.

CHAPTER THIRTEEN

Patti struggled against her captor, but to no avail.

"Calm down," Richard Prescott whispered. "It's me, Mark's father."

She relaxed, and he let her go. "You scared me!" she said.

"I know. I'm sorry. But I figured if I said hi, you'd scream."

He was right, she would have.

"The shooting-gallery man has Mark!" Patti said.

"I know," Mr. Prescott said, then pulled Patti back farther into the shadows. "You need to stay here, hidden. If anyone comes, hightail it out of here."

Alarmed, she asked, "Where are you going?"

"To get my son back."

He was about to step out when someone called for him from the front of the house: "Prescott! We have your son!" Patti recognized the voice. It was the shooting-gallery man.

Mr. Prescott inched his way toward the corner at the front of the house. Patti followed close behind. They both peeked around and saw Mark held fast by the shooting-gallery man and his partner—the one who'd knocked in Mark's bedroom door. They were at the end of the sidewalk by the street. A large, black car with its doors open sat behind them with its engine running.

"You know we don't want to do the boy any harm," the man said. "But we want that bear. Have the girl bring it to the carnival site *alone.* Do you hear? Nobody comes with her. And you'd better not call the police. When we have the bear, you'll get your son back. An even swap. It's that simple. Otherwise . . . well, we can't guarantee what'll happen to the boy."

The two men pushed Mark into the car and, with squealing tires, drove off. Lights came on in some of the houses around the neighborhood. A couple of doors opened as neighbors looked out to see what all the commotion was about. This was *not* normal behavior in Odyssey.

Mr. Prescott leaned against the house and closed his eyes.

"What are we going to do?" Patti asked.

"They won't hurt him," Mr. Prescott said.

"How do you know for sure?"

He looked down at Patti, then poked a finger into the bear. "Because we have what they want. This bear. And I think I know why they want it so badly."

"You do? Why?"

"I can't say right now."

"But what are we going to do about Mark?"

"That depends," Mr. Prescott said solemnly. "How brave are you feeling?"

****

The carnival was dark and desolate. Only a few lights were still on at various points around the site. In the dim glow, the rest of it looked like a junkyard of mangled steel, giant crates, and half-dismantled wooden stalls. Nothing was left to indicate this was supposed to be a *fun* place. It was deathly quiet. *It's spooky and dangerous,* Patti concluded. She wanted to be anywhere but here. She had no choice, though. Mark's life depended on what she did next.

Heart pounding wildly, she slowly walked to the center of the carnival. She swallowed hard, hoping her fear might go away. It didn't. "God, I know I've been really dumb about this whole mess, but please help me now," she prayed.

She looked around to see if anyone was there. The place was empty. She clutched Binger tightly, then quickly loosened her grip, worried that she might damage him. Was she anywhere near where she was supposed to be? No one had told her where she was supposed to go. Would they suddenly leap out at her? She hoped not. Her muscles were wound tight. If anyone appeared, she'd scream and run, whether she meant to or not.

Madam Clara's tent was the most likely place to go. But Patti couldn't remember where it was. She scanned the area for any familiar landmarks—a booth or a ride she'd seen before. Nothing looked right. She kept walking and knew she wasn't really as alone as she felt. She suspected that the shooting-gallery man and his accomplice were watching her from somewhere.

Off to the right, she saw what looked like the remains of the house of horrors. The monsters were gone, but the trailer still had part of the lettering hanging from the top. It read: *H-USE -F H-RR-RS,* as if whoever took it down decided to pack away the O's only.

If she remembered correctly, Madam Clara's tent was nearby. She gave a wide berth to the trailer—not wanting to get too close to any building in case someone tried to grab her—and moved around the small clearing next to it. Madam Clara's tent was there. Flickering candlelight poured out from under the tent's sides and front flap. She thought she saw shadows move within the light.

"Hello?" she called out, her voice sounding stark and loud in the dark silence. She called again, "Is anybody here?"

The tent flap was tossed aside, and Madam Clara stepped out. She seemed shrunken somehow, smaller and stooped. "Hello, child," she said. "You brought the bear?"

"It's here," Patti said and held Binger up for her to see. "You know, you didn't have to take Mark. I was on my way to bring it to you."

Madam Clara snorted. "You took too long. Some of us are impatient."

"I'm impatient, too," Patti said. "Let's get this over with."

"Bring the bear to me," Madam Clara commanded.

Patti pulled Binger close to her and said, "No."

"No?"

"Bring Mark out, and when I see that you're going to let him go, I'll put the bear down right here." Patti spoke carefully and in a steady voice, as if she'd rehearsed the exact words. It was the performance of a lifetime. She was scared out of her wits.

Madam Clara cackled loudly. "You have a lot of spunk considering your predicament, child."

Patti didn't respond but waited and prayed. Madam Clara looked at her for a moment. Then Patti realized that she was talking out of the corner of her mouth to someone inside the tent.

"All right, child," Madam Clara finally said. "But if you try any tricks, you'll regret it." She disappeared into the tent, then returned seconds later with Mark. He was gagged, his hands were bound behind his back, and his feet were tied together, forcing him to hop to get anywhere, or even to stand in place. Patti's heart skipped a beat at the sight of him.

"You see?" the old woman said. "He isn't the worse for wear."

"Let him go and I'll put the bear down," Patti insisted nervously.

"Put the bear down, walk away, and then we'll let him go," the fortune-teller said. "We want to make sure that the bear is . . . *intact.*"

Patti swallowed hard. "No. That's not the deal," she said.

"You're not in a position to bargain, child," Madam Clara said. "You wouldn't want another curse put upon you, would you?"

"I don't believe in you or your curses. You made an idiot

out of me with all that mumbo jumbo, and it won't happen again." Patti pulled a small can of lighter fluid and matches from her jacket pocket. "Let Mark go or I'll burn the bear right here in front of your eyes," she said.

The fortune-teller was visibly surprised. Again, Patti was aware that she began consulting someone in her tent.

Suddenly the shooting-gallery barker stepped out of the tent and roughly grabbed Mark. "I've had enough of this nonsense!" he shouted at Patti, and then he shouted even louder, "I know you're out there somewhere, Prescott! If you know what's good for you—and these two kids—you'll come out now. Come out!"

Patti waited, her blood turning to ice in her veins. *What am I supposed to do now?* she wondered.

"Okay, I'm here," Richard Prescott announced as he came out from behind a half-disassembled salt-and-pepper-shaker ride. He walked toward Patti until he was only a few feet away. "You did a good job," he said softly when he drew near. Speaking even lower, he added, "Get ready to run for cover."

"I want to see that the bear's okay, and *then* you'll get your son," the barker said.

Mr. Prescott took the bear from Patti and slowly made his way toward Madam Clara's tent. "You want the bear?" he said. "You can have it. Here, I'll hand him to you."

"It's a trick," Madam Clara said to the barker.

"Stop where you are," the barker said to Richard Prescott.

"You're going to have to make up your minds," Mr.

Prescott said. "Maybe I can help you."

Patti noticed Mr. Prescott's right hand fall to his side. He clenched his fist. Suddenly the world seemed to explode behind her. She fell to her knees, aware that the salt-and-pepper shaker had erupted. In that same instant, Richard Prescott leaped for the barker and Mark. Madam Clara screamed and ran into the tent. *That must be the signal,* Patti thought and dove for the shell of a nearby stall.

Hiding inside, she lay on the ground, panting heavily. She listened and waited. The previous emptiness of the carnival was taken over by loud crackling and whistles. Mr. Prescott must have rigged the ride somehow or set off a fireworks display, Patti assumed. She had known he was going to do *something* but didn't know what. Men and women shouted from every different direction. "Fire! Fire!" someone yelled over and over.

She wondered what had happened to Mark and his father. Working up some nerve, she peeked over the counter of the stall. Mark lay near the tent, squirming against the ropes that bound him. The bear lay abandoned nearby. Two men—Richard Prescott and the barker?—wrestled in the doorway to the tent. They punched, kicked, and rolled until they disappeared inside.

This was her chance to help Mark, Patti quickly decided, and she raced over to him. Reaching him, she pulled off the electric tape on his mouth.

"Ouch!" he cried, then gasped, "Get my pocket knife."

"Where is it?" she asked.

"In my pocket! Where else?" he cried. He rolled so his right pocket faced up.

She dug in his pocket, pulled out the knife, and cut at his adhesive bonds. Her hands shook so much that she was afraid she'd stab him accidentally.

Just as she freed his hands, Madam Clara appeared out of the shadows and hobbled quickly toward the bear.

"Don't let her get that bear!" Mark shouted.

Patti, without thinking about the danger, sprinted toward the bear, too. It was a neck-and-neck race, but Patti got there first, scooping up the bear.

Madam Clara lunged out and grabbed Patti's hair before she could get away. She yanked Patti back and growled, "Give that to me, you rotten child!"

Patti gave her a hard kick in the shin.

Madam Clara yelped but held fast to Patti's hair. By now Mark had cut the bindings from his legs, and he came running full speed at Madam Clara.

"Let go of her!" he shouted angrily, and an instant later he tackled her with his full weight.

The three of them went down in a confused tangle of flailing arms and kicking legs. Madam Clara clawed at them until they had to roll away from her. Patti was on her knees, clinging to Binger. Mark leaped to his feet.

"I'll scratch your eyes out," the old woman hissed as she got to her feet.

Suddenly the area was filled with a bright, white light. Spotlights hit them from all directions. A voice on a megaphone shouted metallically, "This is the police! Everyone stay where you are! You're completely surrounded!"

Madam Clara shrieked and headed for the clearing behind her tent. A policeman—the same one who'd come to the Eldridges' home—moved toward her from the dark field beyond.

"Not another step," he said to her as he drew his gun.

She swore at him but stopped where she was and held out her arms, certain he would put handcuffs on her wrists.

"You know the routine," Officer Stenson said with a smile as he holstered his gun and took out his handcuffs. Then he obliged her by cuffing her hands behind her back.

"My dad!" Mark shouted and ran to the tent.

Just then, Richard Prescott came out. His shirt was torn, and a trickle of blood slipped from his lip. "I'm all right," he said breathlessly. "But you'll need to call an ambulance for the gentleman inside."

Detective Anderson entered the scene and shouted, "Everyone's going to the police station!" He pointed angrily at Mr. Prescott and added, "And *you* have a lot of explaining to do!"

CHAPTER FOURTEEN

The interrogation room at the Odyssey police station was too small to handle both the Eldridges and the Prescotts, so Detective Anderson moved them into the squad briefing room. It had several rows of chairs, posters and charts on the wall about police reports, and a large blackboard behind a podium.

Mr. and Mrs. Eldridge hovered around their daughter anxiously. “Are you sure you’re okay?” they asked repeatedly.

She assured them she was. In fact, she was more worried about *them.* The car accident had left her father with a black eye and her mother with a large bruise on her arm.

“We look like a casualty center,” Mr. Prescott said as he pressed an ice bag against his lip to help stop the swelling. His forehead was bruised, and the corner of his eye had turned an angry red. Apart from that comment and a lengthy, whispered conversation with an FBI agent at the back of the room, Mr. Prescott had been quiet and subdued.

Mark was also banged up. His wrists were chaffed from the tape with which he'd been bound. He also had two scratches along his left cheek, compliments of Madam Clara's claws. Julie Prescott stayed attentive to Mark and had found some ointment to put on the scratches. "This'll keep them from scarring," she said.

Mark said he wanted the scars. "It'll make me look cool," he said, "like a pirate."

"You're such a *boy,*" Mrs. Prescott complained. "I should have had a daughter."

"They're no easier," Mr. Eldridge said with a wink.

Patti, whose only casualty was a tear in the knee of her jeans, held on to Binger and watched everyone with a feeling of numbness. She was exhausted. But she didn't want to miss anything that was about to happen. Now maybe she would learn some of the answers behind what had been happening to her for the past couple of days.

Detective Anderson burst into the room, letting the door slam behind him. "I'll never work in a small town again!" he said. "I have a dozen people out there to book and nowhere to put them! And those FBI agents won't even let me talk to them! 'Sensitive material,' they keep saying. I guess Madam Clara and her gang are stumbling all over themselves confessing and trying to make a deal to get off light." He threw his overcoat aside and abruptly snatched up a pot of coffee from a nearby table. Making sure it was warm, he poured some into a plastic mug. "Anybody want some?" he asked.

They'd all had their fill and said no, thanks.

The detective pulled up a chair and sat in front of them. "Do you know how stupid that scheme was?" he demanded. "You never should have gone out to the carnival like that without calling me first."

"I called you," Julie Prescott corrected him.

"Fifteen minutes *later,*" he complained. "Somebody could've been seriously hurt."

Patti appreciated the detective's complaint, but everything had happened so fast. After the shooting-gallery man—whose name turned out to be Fred Barber—and his sidekick drove away with Mark, Richard Prescott had gone back into the house and made some quick calls. Patti wasn't sure who all the people were that he talked to, but she could tell they were in the government. After getting the okay from them to work his plan, he'd told Patti that she'd have to take the bear to the carnival, but only if she was up to it. She had said she was.

By then, Julie Prescott had returned with Mr. and Mrs. Eldridge. They talked everything over. Mr. Prescott hadn't gone into details then, but he was sure he wasn't dealing with killer criminals. They were amateurs, he had said. He was certain they wouldn't hurt Mark or Patti. They just wanted the bear.

"What's so important about that blasted bear?" Mr. Eldridge had asked.

Mr. Prescott had shaken his head and said he couldn't explain. He went on to his plan, which was simple: Patti would take the bear to Madam Clara's tent—they figured that was the most likely place—while Richard Prescott and several agents from an FBI field office in Connellsville followed from various points around Brook Meadow.

"It's somewhat risky," Mr. Prescott had said, "but we don't have many options."

Patti and her parents had agreed to go along with it.

"Just so they get what's coming to them for all this trouble," Mr. Eldridge had said.

It was then that Patti had learned how Mr. Prescott had made a lot of mental notes about the layout of the carnival when he had gone to visit it with Patti's father. That's how he knew the fireworks were stored near the salt-and-pepper-shaker ride. It was a gamble—and fortunate—that the fireworks hadn't been moved yet during the packing-up process.

The only thing about the plan that didn't make sense to Patti was the very thing Detective Anderson had complained about: Mr. Prescott had insisted that no one call the Odyssey police until they had a good head start to get to the carnival. That's why the police showed up when they did.

"No offense, detective," Richard Prescott now explained, "but it's *because* this is a small-town police force that I didn't think it was a good idea to involve you from the start."

Detective Anderson was indignant. "Do you know where I came from?" he said. "Chicago. Fifteen years I worked as a detective on a big-city force. And let me tell you that if you'd done this in Chicago, I'd have your rear end in jail. I don't care who you're an agent for!"

"An agent!" Mrs. Eldridge exclaimed.

"You're an agent?" Patti asked, her mouth dropping. She looked at Mark accusingly. "Mark!"

"I'm not allowed to talk about my dad's job," Mark replied.

Mr. Prescott held up his hand. "I'm not an *agent* of anything," he insisted. "I work as a consultant with a couple of the intelligence agencies. That's all."

"They must have trained you to be more than a consultant," the detective said sarcastically.

"It's true. We're trained to be prepared for things like this. One never knows when spies and traitors might try something foolish. I just never expected it to happen in Odyssey."

"Spies and traitors!" Mr. Eldridge said. "You'd better explain yourself, Richard."

Mr. Prescott nodded and said, "I'll go back to the beginning. I told you that the government complex is going to be a site for archives, computers, and information."

"A big filing cabinet," Patti said, echoing her father's statement from before.

"Right. What I didn't say was *which* part of the government it's connected to. In fact, I still can't say precisely. But it's enough for you to know that it has to do with some of our intelligence and security agencies."

Mrs. Eldridge asked, "You mean the complex is going to hold *top secret* information?"

"Yep," Mark's father said. "It's designed to be an information clearinghouse and think tank for those agencies."

"But . . . in Odyssey?" Mr. Eldridge asked in disbelief.

Mr. Prescott shrugged. "Why not? Their work doesn't require them to be in the Washington area. But the main reason is that Odyssey is in a beautifully *remote* part of the country."

Detective Anderson sipped his coffee, then said, "Okay, so the complex was supposed to be top secret, and you're a top-secret consultant. I'm impressed. But that doesn't explain what's been going on here."

"Yeah. Why have those carnival people been trying to drive me crazy?" Patti asked.

"Because they made a big mistake."

Again, they were all surprised. "What kind of mistake?" Patti's father asked.

Mr. Prescott stood up and paced as he spoke. "They let Patti win the bear at the shooting gallery, and she wasn't the one who was supposed to get it. As I said, they made a mistake. Rather, *Madam Clara* made a mistake."

"But how did they make the mistake?" Mr. Eldridge asked.

"We're still not sure," Mr. Prescott replied. "For some reason, Madam Clara thought Patti was her contact to get the bear. It was obviously a two-step process to keep from getting caught. Madam Clara was supposed to make sure it was the right girl and then give her the playing card—the queen of hearts. Then the girl was to give the card to Fred Barber as a signal to let her win the bear. Imagine their surprise when they realized Patti *wasn't* their contact! But she had the bear now, and they had to figure out how to get it back."

Mr. Eldridge asked, "Contact for *who,* though?"

"We don't know yet. In fact, Madam Clara wasn't even sure, which was why she made her mistake."

"So all the trouble we've had has been because of them trying to get the bear?" Mrs. Eldridge asked, amazed.

"Uh huh."

She looked perplexed, then asked, "But how did they know where to look? Patti never told them her name."

Mr. Prescott turned to Patti and said, "You said they saw you drive away from the carnival. My guess is that they got your license plate number, had the means to get your address and details, and started after the bear right away."

"So they ransacked our house for it," Mr. Eldridge said.

"And they couldn't find it," said Mr. Prescott.

"He was in the trunk of the car!" said Patti as she suddenly remembered.

Mr. Prescott nodded. "They couldn't know that. They also didn't dare break into your car while you were in public places like Whit's End, the church—"

"Or the diner," Julie Prescott said. "Remember when we saw that man by the car?"

They all nodded as the memory came back. Patti wondered if the shooting-gallery man was trying to sneak a peek to see if the bear was in the car itself.

Mr. Prescott continued, "They *did* get something from your house, though. Mark's letter. It had our last name and address on it. People on the inside know that I've been working on this project. The letter was an important link between Patti and me—a bonus for them. They thought they could use it to their advantage."

"I still don't understand something," Mr. Eldridge said. "Why did Madam Clara go to Whit's End—and what was behind that whole business about the curse?"

"I'm sorry to say that Patti set herself up for that." Mr. Prescott glanced apologetically at Patti. "Once Madam Clara realized her cohorts couldn't get the bear from your house, she had to come up with another plan to get the bear—preferably from you. So she played on your superstition to manipulate you."

Patti blushed but didn't say anything.

"Once she had you believing you were cursed, she let her pals do things to shake you up. I'm sure if you think back to everything that's happened over the past few days—Madam Clara at the window, the fire at Trickle Lake, the brakes going out on the car—you'll see that you weren't cursed. You were simply being followed and harassed. And leaving those playing cards was a shrewd way to remind you of her warning. The more frightened you were, the easier it was to get you to bring the bear to her."

"But she never asked me to bring Binger to her," Patti said, as if it might let her off the hook somehow.

"She didn't? Are you sure?"

Patti thought back to their encounter in the diner rest room. She blushed even deeper. "Well . . . in a way she made me think that *I* decided to do it."

Mark's father smiled sympathetically at her. "Don't feel

bad, Patti," he said. "Madam Clara makes her living as a fortune-teller. That means she's a fake, but she has to be a *good* fake. And that means she has to know how to twist people's thinking around. She played mind games with you from the very start."

"She made me look like an idiot," Patti said sourly. "I still feel like one."

Mr. Eldridge couldn't resist a quick fatherly lecture. "But if you'd been honest with us all along, we could have set you straight," he said. "You *know* not to believe in things like bad luck, fortune-telling, or curses. If you'd held on to what you believe from the Bible, you wouldn't have been fooled."

Mark raised his hand as if he were in class. "Wait a minute, Dad," he said. "You still haven't told us why they had to get the bear back."

"A very good question, young man," Detective Anderson said. "Why in the world is a stuffed bear so important—and worth taking all these risks?"

"Because of what's inside him." Mr. Prescott gestured to Binger and said, "If we rip him open, I suspect we'll find a few surprises. Does anybody have a knife?"

"I do!" Mark exclaimed, then dug in his pockets. Disappointment fell across his face. "Oh, no, I think I lost it at the carnival!"

"I have one," Detective Anderson said, and he stood up to pull it from his pocket. "Hand me the bear and I'll do the honors."

Mr. Prescott reached a hand out to Patti. "May I?"

Patti playfully resisted giving him the bear. "Aw, are you really going to hurt Binger?" she asked.

"He won't feel a thing," Mr. Prescott promised with a smile.

At that moment, a man in a suit opened the door. He had the professional look of an FBI agent rather than one of Odyssey's own police officers.

"Excuse me," he said to Detective Anderson, "but we caught this girl wandering around the building. She claims she's your daughter."

"Kim is here?" the detective asked, surprised.

The man in the suit stepped aside so they could see the girl. Patti recognized her instantly, though she now wore a smart-looking jogging outfit and her hair was stylishly brushed, not stuck under a baseball cap.

"Kim!" the detective cried out happily.

"Hi, Daddy." The girl looked at the crowd of people uneasily. "I'm sorry. I didn't mean to interrupt. I came down with a snack for you. I put it on the desk in your office."

Detective Anderson gave her a hug. "Thanks," he said. "I'd introduce you to everyone, but we're a little busy right now. See you later."

"Bye." The girl quickly walked out, and the man closed the door again.

"Where were we?" the detective said, then remembered. "The bear."

Mr. Prescott reached to take the bear from Patti.

She pulled it tighter as an odd feeling of doubt came over

her. "No, Mr. Prescott," she said very seriously.

He looked at her, puzzled. "What?"

"Something's wrong," she said. Her mind was working fast as the doubt suddenly grew. But she was unsure of where to go with it. She needed a minute to think.

"What's wrong?" Mr. Prescott asked.

"Give him the bear, Patti," her father insisted.

Detective Anderson came over to her, his hand also out. "Let me have it, Patti. We'll put an end to this mystery and go home. It's late." He leaned toward her. The gun in his shoulder holster peeked out from under his suit jacket.

"No," she said more loudly. She sounded panicked, though she wasn't. "I have to think about this."

"Think about what?" Detective Anderson demanded.

Patti looked wide-eyed up at Mr. Prescott. There was something about the girl—who she was and what she said. It didn't line up. Then it clicked. "It's Detective Anderson," she said. "He's the contact."

Detective Anderson turned beet red. "What did you say?" he asked.

Mr. Prescott scrutinized Patti. "You'd better explain yourself," he said.

"That girl—I'm not sure, but how can she be his daughter?" She looked to her parents and said, "Don't you remember? He came to the house and said he was up at all hours because he was a bachelor."

Mrs. Eldridge thought about it, then nodded. "That's right," she confirmed. "He did."

"A bachelor can have a daughter from a previous marriage, can't he? I'm a widower!" he said emphatically.

Patti hadn't thought of that, but it wasn't the only thing that bothered her. Her voice began to rise in pitch as she spoke. "But that girl. I saw her at the carnival. We bumped into each other. It surprised me because we looked so much alike."

"I was going to say that she looked like she could be your sister," Mrs. Eldridge said.

"The other day, she was dressed just like I was, and it made her look almost like my twin. Then I saw her later with Madam Clara when we were driving away!" The image was fixed in her mind now—and the truth came clear.

"What does that have to do with anything?" Detective Anderson said. "A lot of people went to the carnival!"

"Madam Clara thought I was that girl," Patti said to the detective. That was it in a nutshell. Detective Anderson was the missing piece: the contact who was supposed to get the bear filled with whatever secrets it held inside.

Detective Anderson suddenly laughed at her. "This is ridiculous!" he said, but he quickly pulled his gun out from under his jacket. "Now stand back," he barked at Mr. Prescott.

Mr. Prescott rolled his eyes in exasperation. "I never would have suspected you," he said.

"But you suspected *someone* on the police force, didn't you?" the detective replied.

"I knew someone with the local police was involved with

Madam Clara's gang because they got the license number details so quickly."

Detective Anderson sneered. "That's why you didn't want the police at the carnival right away."

"Now I know why you couldn't seem to help us," Mr. Eldridge added. "You didn't want to."

"You also showed up at Whit's End the night Madam Clara was there," Mrs. Eldridge said, as if she were just catching on to the game of "Accuse Detective Anderson."

"Yes, yes, you're all very clever," the detective said impatiently. "But I can't stick around to listen to the rest of your Agatha Christie impressions. Give me that bear and I'll go." His eyes darted toward the main door, then over to an emergency exit on the opposite wall.

Patti held on to Binger.

Detective Anderson pointed the gun at her. "That bear is worth a lot of money. Give him to me."

"He's worthless," Mr. Prescott said. "You have to realize that the project has been compromised. We'll change everything. Whatever information is in that bear is useless to you now."

"Is it? You're going to tell me that the architectural plans for the government complex are no good?"

"The government complex won't be built. Not here. Not now."

Detective Anderson chuckled. "But these plans aren't for this complex alone. Your design for this building was used for embassies and complexes all over the world. Don't you think that would be worth something? Don't you think there are groups and organizations who'd pay a lot of money to see the top-secret designs of intelligence buildings in, say, the Middle East or Russia or South America?"

The blood drained from Richard Prescott's face. He didn't reply.

"Just as I thought," the detective said. He reached down and grabbed Binger by the neck. His gun pointed at Patti, he growled, "Let go."

Patti did.

Keeping his eye on everyone in the room, the detective backed toward the door. He pushed the bar down behind him and shoved the door open. Cool night air blew in.

"You won't get far," Mr. Prescott said.

"I'll get far enough," Detective Anderson said. "My daughter's 'message' was her way of telling me that certain things were in place for us to leave. I needed this bear and—"

Suddenly he froze where he was, his face awash with surprise.

A voice behind him said, "Freeze. Drop the gun."

The detective obeyed. The gun rattled as it hit the floor. Richard Prescott quickly walked over and grabbed it up.

"And the bear," the voice said.

Detective Anderson handed the bear to Mr. Prescott.

"Now, get down on the floor, face down, with your arms and legs spread. You know how it's done."

Again, the detective obeyed. As he did, the door swung open wide, and John Avery Whittaker stepped inside. He wasn't holding a gun at all. He had pressed a large pen against the detective's back. He blew on the end like an old cowboy who'd just won a gunfight, then slipped the pen back into his shirt pocket. "Imagine my surprise when I was walking past the station and saw Detective Anderson waving a gun around," he said. "I thought, *Now that's strange, what could he be up to?*"

"Thanks, Whit," Mr. Prescott said. "Bob, would you get Agent Cooper in here?"

Mr. Eldridge nodded, then rushed into the hallway to bring in the FBI.

From the floor, Detective Anderson groaned. "I want my lawyer!" he demanded.

"In time," Richard Prescott said. He handed Whit the bear and told him, "You'd better get this out of here before anyone else decides to try for it."

"Okay," Mr. Whittaker said and took the bear.

Expressions of disbelief fell like shadows across every face around the room.

"You work for the government, too?" Mark cried out.

Mr. Whittaker shrugged and smiled. "It's a hobby," he said.

As quickly as he had appeared, he disappeared back through the door.

CHAPTER FIFTEEN

It wasn't until the next day, when the Eldridges and Prescotts reunited for lunch, that Richard explained to them about Mr. Whittaker. "He's given me the okay to say only this much: He's worked as an analyst and researcher for the government off and on for years. Because he was local, I was instructed to ask him to find out what was inside the bear, then hold onto it for safekeeping—or to make certain that it's destroyed. He came to the station to get the bear. Fortunately, he came when he did."

Patti shook her head. There was still so much she didn't know about Mr. Whittaker.

"What will happen to Detective Anderson, Madam Clara, and the rest?" Mr. Eldridge asked.

"The FBI has them all in custody. They'll go to trial and, hopefully, will be prosecuted as the traitors they are. You won't be asked to testify in person, by the way. They'll videotape your testimonies."

Patti was genuinely surprised. It hadn't occurred to her that she might have to make a court appearance.

"We'll do anything we can to help," Mr. Eldridge said.

"Thank you," Mark's father said. "And I hope I don't have to say too strongly that you can't talk about any of this. To anyone. You have to pretend it didn't happen. If word got out, there'd be no end of problems."

They all agreed soberly.

Mr. Prescott looked uncomfortable for a moment, then said, "I got some other bad news, though. Julie and Mark don't even know about this."

Everyone waited with hardly a breath between them.

"As I suggested in the confrontation with Detective Anderson, as far as the government is concerned, the site has been compromised. They said we'll have to draw up new plans and choose a different place to build it. Now they're saying they want it *closer* to Washington."

"Oh, no," Patti said as she realized what that meant. Mark wouldn't be moving back to Odyssey after all. Patti exchanged sad glances with Mark. He then sat quietly and stared at the table.

That wasn't the end of it. "I'm really sorry, but I have to go back to Washington right away," he added.

"Today?" Julie Prescott asked.

"I have to give a full report about what happened and pull together the teams to discuss our change in plans." He looked miserable and said again, "I'm sorry, everyone. I didn't expect this to happen."

Lunch was ruined for Patti and Mark. They ate quickly and quietly.

"We could let your father go home and fly back later in the week," Julie Prescott suggested to Mark.

"No," he pouted, "I don't want to be here if we're not moving back. Why torture ourselves?"

Later in the afternoon, when Patti was alone with Mark on her front porch, she said, "You know, you're getting a little too big to pout like that. You could've hung around for the rest of the week. We could do things together, have fun."

Mark shook his head. "I know it sounds crazy," he said, "but if I stay and have fun and get used to going to Whit's End and . . . and being with you . . . then I'll be miserable when I have to go back to Washington. Maybe I'm being a brat, but I don't know how to have a good time here and then be happy back there."

Patti thought about it for a few minutes as they looked out at the beautiful spring day. Somewhere, someone had started a lawnmower. A bird sang nearby. "We have to try harder, Mark."

"Try *what* harder?" Mark asked.

"Try to get used to where we are," she said. Her mother's words came back to her. "We have to get on with our lives."

Mark frowned at her. "That's easy for you to say," he challenged. "You're living here in Odyssey."

She frowned back at him. "What makes you think it's easy? For a long time after you left, I didn't like Odyssey. I hated it."

"How could you hate Odyssey?" he asked incredulously.

"Because *you* weren't here! Are you completely clueless? I *miss you,* you clod! You're the closest friend I've ever had, and I hate it when you're not around. But I have to try. *We* have to try. It's wrong to be miserable."

Mark sat quietly for a moment. "I miss you, too," he finally said softly.

"I love you, Mark," Patti whispered quickly before she lost her nerve.

He didn't look at her. He stared at his fingers as they folded and unfolded nervously on his lap. "I love you, too," he whispered back.

Patti didn't know if he understood what she meant by those words, or if he understood what he meant when he responded. She didn't dare press him. She left the moment alone.

The Prescotts were ready to depart later that afternoon. Mark reluctantly hugged Patti before he left.

"Maybe we'll come back this summer!" Julie Prescott said hopefully.

Then they were gone.

That evening, Patti climbed onto a stool at Whit's End and dejectedly asked Mr. Whittaker for a soda.

"Mark's gone again, huh?" he asked as he handed her the drink.

"Uh huh," she said. She had decided she'd try to get on with her life, but she knew it wouldn't be easy.

"I have something that might help you whenever you

miss Mark," Mr. Whittaker said, reaching under the counter. He lifted up Binger and handed him to her.

"Mr. Whittaker!" she exclaimed, her breath taken away. Binger looked at her with the same melancholy expression he'd always had. Except for a tiny stitch along his back, he looked unchanged.

"I tried to be careful when I worked on him," he said. "I hope you still want him."

"Are you kidding? Thank you, Mr. Whittaker! This is great!" She hugged Binger tightly and swung back and forth on the stool.

Mr. Whittaker observed, "He can never replace a real friend, but he might be nice to have around."

Patti smiled. "He'll do just fine," she said.

"I'm sure he will—until something better comes along," Mr. Whittaker said with a smile and a knowing tone. Then he looked beyond Patti to the door.

Donna Barclay had just walked in. "Hi, Patti," she said. "I just called your house, and your parents said you had come here. I was wondering if you want to go up to Trickle Lake with me. I have to collect leaf samples for a project that's due next week. But only if you want to."

Patti glanced at Mr. Whittaker, then back at Donna. "Only if I want to?" she said. "I'd love to."

About the Author

Paul McCusker is producer, writer, and director for the *Adventures in Odyssey* audio series. He is also the author of a variety of popular plays including *The First Church of Pete's Garage, Pap's Place,* and co-author of *Sixty-Second Skits* (with Chuck Bolte).

Don't Miss a Single "Adventures in Odyssey" Novel!

The Stranger's Message (#11)

What would Jesus do? When a destitute man collapses in front of the kids at Whit's End, that's the very question they agree to ask themselves before making *any* decision. But God's will is not always easy to figure out. After all, the Bible doesn't include verses on having it out with town bullies or blowing the whistle on a bribe-accepting school official. Or does it?

Freedom Run (#10)

When their Imagination Station adventure is cut short, Matt and Jack plead with Whit to let them return to the pre-Civil War South. But what awaits them is even more perilous than before! Through a whirlwind of events, the cast of *Dark Passage* is reunited for a treacherous journey through history along the Underground Railroad.

Dark Passage (#9)

When Matt and Jack discover a trap door in the yard at Whit's End, their curiosities get the best of them as The Imagination Station leads the pair back in time to the pre-Civil War South! And after Matt is mistaken for a runaway slave and sold at an auction, it's up to Jack to find and rescue him!

Point of No Return (#8)

Turning over a new leaf isn't as easy as Jimmy Barclay thought it would be. And when his friends abandon him, his grandmother falls ill, and the only kid who seems to understand what he's going through moves away, he begins to wonder, *Does God really care?* Through the challenges, Jimmy discovers that standing up for what you believe in can be costly—and rewarding!

Danger Lies Ahead (#7)

Jack Davis knew he was off to a bad start when he saw a moving van in front of Mark's house, heard that an escaped convict could be headed toward Odyssey, and found himself in the principal's office—all on the first day of school! Thrown headfirst into the course of chaos, Jack lets his imagination run overtime. Will it cost him his friendships with Oscar and Lucy?

The King's Quest (#6)

Mark is surprised and upset to find he must move back to Washington, D. C. He feels like running away. And that's exactly what The Imagination Station enables him to do! With Whit's help, he goes on a quest for the king to retrieve a precious ring. Through the journey, Mark faces his fears and learns the importance of obeying authority and striving for eternal things.

Lights Out at Camp What-a-Nut (#5)

At camp, Mark finds out he's in the same cabin with Joe Devlin, Odyssey's biggest bully. And when Mark and Joe are paired in a treasure hunt, they plunge into unexpected danger and discover how God uses one person to help another.

Behind the Locked Door (#4)

Why does Mark's friend Whit keep his attic door locked? What's hidden up there? While staying with Whit, Mark grows curious when he's forbidden to go behind the locked door. It's a hard-learned lesson about trust and honesty.

The Secret Cave of Robinwood (#3)

Mark promises his friend Patti he will never reveal the secret of her hidden cave. But when a gang Mark wants to join is looking for a new clubhouse, Mark thinks of the cave. Will he risk his friendship with Patti? Through the adventure, Mark learns about the need to belong and the gift of forgiveness.

High Flyer with a Flat Tire (#2)

Joe Devlin has accused Mark of slashing the tire on his new bike. Mark didn't do it, but how can he prove his innocence? Only by finding the real culprit! With the help of his wise friend, Whit, Mark untangles the mystery and learns new lessons about friendship and family ties.

Strange Journey Back (#1)

Mark Prescott hates being a newcomer in the small town of Odyssey. And he's not too thrilled about his only new friend being a girl. That is, until Patti tells him about a time machine at Whit's End called The Imagination Station. With hopes of using the machine to bring his separated parents together again, Mark learns a valuable lesson about friendship and responsibility.

Other Works by the Author

NOVELS:

Strange Journey Back (Focus on the Family)
High Flyer with a Flat Tire (Focus on the Family)
Secret Cave of Robinwood (Focus on the Family)
Behind the Locked Door (Focus on the Family)
Lights Out at Camp What-a-Nut (Focus on the Family)
The King's Quest (Focus on the Family)
Danger Lies Ahead (Focus on the Family)
Point of No Return (Focus on the Family)
Dark Passage (Focus on the Family)
Freedom Run (Focus on the Family)
The Stranger's Message (Focus on the Family)
Catacombs (Tyndale)
Time Twists: Sudden Switch (Chariot/Lion)
Time Twists: Stranger in the Mist (Chariot/Lion)
Time Twists: Memory's Gate (Chariot/Lion)
You Say Tomato (with Adrian Plass; HarperCollins UK)

INSTRUCTIONAL:

Playwriting:
A Study in Choices & Challenges (Lillenas)

SKETCH COLLECTIONS:

Batteries Not Included (Baker's Plays)
Fast Foods (Monarch UK)
Drama for Worship, Vol. 1: On the Street Interview (Word)
Drama for Worship, Vol. 2: The Prodigal & the Pig Farmer (Word)
Drama for Worship, Vol. 3: Complacency (Word)
Drama for Worship, Vol. 4: Conversion (Word)
Quick Skits and Discussion Starters (with Chuck Bolte; Group Books)
Sixty-Second Skits (with Chuck Bolte; Group Books)
Short Skits for Youth Ministry (with Chuck Bolte; Group Books)
Sketches of Harvest (Baker's Plays)
Souvenirs (Baker's Plays)
Vantage Points (Lillenas)
Void Where Prohibited (Baker's Plays)

PLAYS:

The Case of the Frozen Saints (Baker's Plays)
The First Church of Pete's Garage (Baker's Plays)
The Revised Standard Version of Jack Hill (Baker's Plays)
A Work in Progress (Lillenas)
Camp W (CDS)
Catacombs (Lillenas)

Death by Chocolate (Baker's Plays)
Family Outings (Lillenas)
Father's Anonymous (Lillenas)
Pap's Place (Lillenas)
Snapshots & Portraits (Lillenas)

MUSICALS:

The Meaning of Life & Other Vanities (with Tim Albritton; Baker's Plays)
Shine the Light of Christmas (with Dave and Jan Williamson; Word Music)
A Time for Christmas (with David Clydesdale, Steve Amerson, Lowell Alexander; Word Music)